Terramara:
Mara's Transformation

Kris Fuller

Enjoy my book and follow your dreams! Hugs from Kris Fuller

WALDORF PUBLISHING

Published by Waldorf Publishing
2140 Hall Johnson Road
#102-345
Grapevine, Texas 76051
www.WaldorfPublishing.com

Terramara : Mara's Transformation

ISBN: 978-1-64921-463-8

Library of Congress Control Number: 2020940365

Copyright © 2020

Design by Baris Celik

Dedication

For my loving husband, Ben.

Contents

Prologue... 1

1 Marhilias... 3

2 Mara and Aida 5

3 The Mountains of Mardivina 7

4 Thirsty Raccoons 10

5 The Plains of Zulta 13

6 The Caves of Decault... 15

7 Sandy Bend 17

8 The Great Falls 19

9 Human Prince 21

10 The Top of the Falls 24

11 Cyrus's Dive.. 27

12 Concern.. 30

13 Mara 32

14 Return to the Palace.. 34

15 Aida's Discovery 37

16 Cyrus's Thoughts 39

17 Connection 40

18 The Meeting 44

19 Still Waters 49

20 The Library 53

21 The Visit 55

22 Blue Crystals 56

23 To The River 59

24 Change 62

25 The Gifts 64

26 New Terrain 66

27 Warm Welcome 70

28 New Friends 75

29 The Palace.. 81

30 The King 83

31 Farewell.. 86

32 The Invitation 91

33 The Bad News 93

34 An Explanation 95

35 The Visit 101

36 Preparing 104

37 The Celebration 106

38 White Columns 108

39 The Heart of the River 110

40 Forged.. 113

41 Watering Changes... 115

42 Watering 117

Author Bio 118

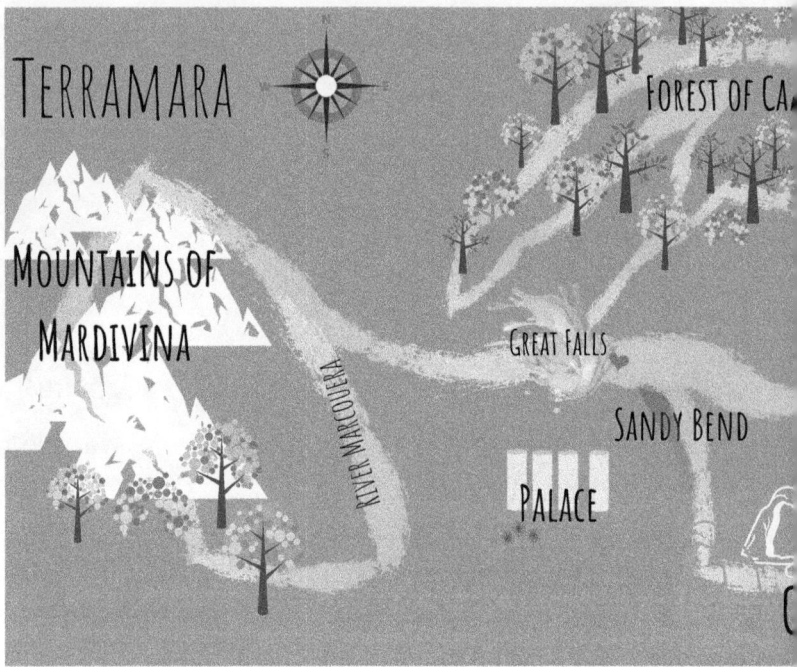

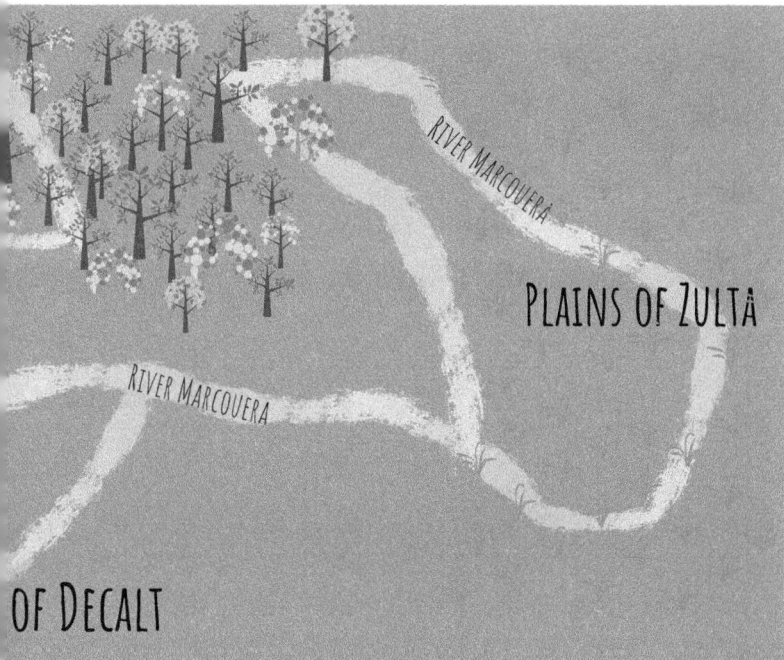

RIVER MARCOUERA

PLAINS OF ZULTÄ

RIVER MARCOUERA

OF DECALT

Prologue

At one time, the great kingdom known as Terramara was called Elementia and it was governed by three magical beings, each harnessing a unique element. Fierana ruled fire, Marcouera ruled water, and Terraina ruled earth. The rulers were like sisters. Balance and peace existed for thousands of years.

That is, of course, until a king from the human world lusted after the power of fire. He sent spies, thieves and sorcerers into the far corners of the land. He raged wars against all the elements and their queens. He was relentless in his goal.

The enchantress's powers and their connections to each other began to fray, each scrambling to save her own domain at the expense of the others. The elements were unrelenting, hurting those they had once considered to be their sisters. Battles began to wear down the magical connection of the enchanted three. As they slowly unraveled, one by one, their elements raged and caused great harm to the land.

First came the fires that burned for one hundred nights and days. Fierana's anguish and fury was hard to bear and impossible to stop.

Terraina battled the scorching flames as long as she could, weakening both her land and her powers so much that she was powerless to protect herself from her true enemy: the king. Her efforts were not unnoticed, for Elementia *shifted* under her command and stunning white rock formations appeared in the center and the west of Elementia. With the rise of those stones, the first sister fell to her fate. The rocks slowed the fires, but at a great cost.

Devastated, Marcouera knew she was the last hope to stop the fires. It would be the end of Fierana and she was unsure what it would mean for her. She drew every last ounce of strength to call forth the rivers and flood the lands.

When the waters calmed, the fires were extinguished and the evil king drowned. However, this brave act took so much of her power, she could no longer feel the bond with her sisters and became incredibly weak.

Marcouera, the last of the Goddesses to fall, gave her final watery breath to create a chance for the world to survive. With one last burst of magic, she split her spirit into a million pieces of tiny water droplets, then sank to the bottom of the river's heart, a small shred of what she once was.

These enchanted droplets would allow the world to live.

1 Marhilias

Whoosh!

The river Marcouera leapt and skipped over the Great Falls. Thousands of tiny marhilias giggled with glee as they rode the sparkling blue river around the land of Terramara.

Marhilias blended into any body of water they came in contact with. They splashed in and out of the river, amongst all living things, leaving dew and water in their paths. They were difficult to see with the naked eye. Their watery compositions made a small refraction of light, a tiny rainbow when sunlight touched them. They had minuscule bodies, the size of a large raindrop, silvery and delicate. Their entire being was made up of water, allowing them to separate into a million tiny droplets and merge back together whenever they desired. A marhilia can never be trapped.

Humans cannot hear marhilias. When they speak to one another, it sounds only as a soft murmur. (It's difficult to distinguish the sound between rushing water and magical sprites.)

The river *calls* to all marhilias. No matter where they journeyed in this great land, they can always feel and hear the river. No human can hear the river's call. It's an ancient, magical hum. The call gently seeped from the heart of the river and kept every sprite connected to one another.

The River Marcouera was unlike any other river in the world. It sent out tributaries and branches, as all rivers do, but what made Marcouera special was this: it flowed in *both* directions at the *same* time. Each branch wove to and from the mighty main river; and through this magic the marhilias could travel anywhere in Terramara at any time.

The marhilias kept the world of Terramara green and thriving. These harmonious creatures left splashes of dew and drips of water wherever they go. They glided in and out of the river, sharing their unlimited source of water. They bounded off blades of grass, flowers, and fields, leaving dew and droplets behind. Always watering, always moving.

Marhilias were part of the river, with the freedom to travel in and out of it as they pleased. Two such marhilias who cherished watery adventures in Terramara were Mara and Aida.

2 Mara and Aida

"Mara! Hurry up!" laughed Aida. "Let's go!"

Mara was just behind her friend, riding the rushing rapids.

"I'm coming!" Mara yelled above the thundering river. "I want to visit the flowers in the morning."

"Sure thing," Aida smiled back. "That way, we can finish our day at the falls!"

Aida found a twisting current and let herself spin around for a few moments. Mara stood on top of a small wave and laughed freely at her friend. She knew Aida was enjoying herself.

All marhilias shimmered in the sunlight. Aida's shimmer of orange was brighter than any other color. It was warm and soft. Mara loved that summery glint, it almost seemed to glow when Aida was excited.

Mara stood on the river's surface, surfing beside her friend. Each ripple sent them spinning and twisting. They challenged one another to balancing acts and tricks. Aida flipped over a wave. Mara smiled and answered with a backflip. They jumped, bounced, and created ripples as they flowed with the river. They rode the Quick Current for a while, then skated over to the Slow Side. Any rapids that were *excellent* for tricks often got two, or even three returns, before they moved along.

Aida coasted for a moment and watched her friend's sheer joy. She thought about how wonderful their watery world was. Mara flipped and disappeared from view. Did she fall in? Aida squinted, having lost sight of her for a moment, but then smiled as she came back into focus. (Mara may have fallen, but it would never hurt. She would simply pop up again and continue with the water.)

The water and Mara were so similar. Mara's shimmers were mainly silver and blue. Yes, yes, she had the oranges, reds, and purples in her twinkly mix as well but, oh, those blues! So many *distinct* shades. Aida admired Mara's jewel-toned appearance, noticing the gorgeous hues of sapphire, silver, and aquamarine. They twinkled at her as Mara did her next set of tricks, squealing with joy. Mara skipped over to the Quick Current and was whisked towards the east again.

Not wanting to be idle any longer, Aida somersaulted forward then skidded into that same current. Before long, she had caught up to Mara's watery circle.

3 The Mountains of Mardivina

They veered west to the Mountains of Mardivina.

'Mara! Come on!' Aida called.

'I'm coming!' Mara smiled knowingly. She knew what was next!

They skipped into the Quick Current and raced. Surfing on their watery bases, Aida was tucked inside the barrel of a wave, just in front of her friend. Mara was on another current, equally fast, moments behind. Both were grinning and enjoying the challenge.

The river quickened. Both sprites were lifted inches above the water, their shape now looking like a stretched droplet, hovering and racing along.

Their speed was incredible. They picked up momentum within the rapids and before long, the embankment changed. They were at the base of the mountains surrounded by smooth, white marble, and silver rocks.

The sprites trembled with excitement as the river's magic was strong. The Quick Current was the *quickest* here; it pushed and drove itself up, up, up! Climbing the mountain with magical force, carving in and out of croded rocks, the water sprites zigged and zagged at an incredible speed.

Without a word, both girls left the surface, choosing to dive in. Encompassed by water, they powered upward in the midst of hundreds of other marhilias. They bounced and bumped into one another. Despite speed, no injury occurred. They continued to race up, up, up. White caps, spray, and foam frothed around both sides of the pearly embankments.

The Slow Side was much smaller here, softly

meandering down. It gently trickled down the mountain with no effort at all. A handful of marhilias were coasting down this Slow Side, a more peaceful ride. Aida and Mara whistled past their cohorts, fellow marhilia's were blurs of color at this speed.

Rays of sunlight bounced off the river onto the mountainside. Suddenly, they arrived at the summit. The great river took a breath and steadied itself for the journey around and down the other side. As it slowed, the sprites hopped off and flitted across a smooth ledge. Dewdrops and tiny pools were formed in the rocks where they touched down. A crew of marhilias danced on this ledge for a moment, taking in the sights.

Aida and Mara skipped a little further away then held still. Looking across the great lands below, they could see the entire length of the river across Terramara.

Well, that's not entirely true. It wasn't that they could 'see' it, it was more like they could 'feel' it. They could feel the curves and currents of the river from way up here. The girls could sense how clear the water was on the east side. They knew how fast the Quick Current was in the Plains of Zulta and they knew how many marhilias were in the Cazmal forest. The water spirit that all marhilias shared was clear and precise at the mountain top.

Eventually, they returned to the river and started the lazy journey down on the back side. As they said goodbye to the last of the silver rocks, lush grasses and tiny bright flowers took over the scene. Mara smiled. This was her favorite place.

Mara watched flowers go by in a blur of vibrant color as she sailed down. She constantly flitted over the banks and onto petals, leaves, and stems. The flowers always perked right up when she crashed into them. Sometimes, it felt like the flowers could sense her coming- they would lean into the direction she bounded from and ensure a steady landing.

Mara was too light to hurt any living thing. Even at her fastest, the flowers would feel no more than if rain droplets were falling on them. The droplets Mara left behind were what they craved, what they needed to survive. It seldom rained in Terramara, but it didn't matter to the gardens and the people. The river and marhilias kept everything alive.

4 Thirsty Raccoons

The sprites left the last of the flowers. They passed the Great Falls and headed north. A quick branch of the river rushed through the forest of Cazmal. The two friends swirled along on small, wild currents.

"Woo-hoo!" hollered Aida as she shot into the trees.

Mara yelled back as she was launched to a small branch, "Woo-hoo!"

The Quick Current here was a bit erratic, it tossed them this way and that way as it wove between grand trees.

The forest of Cazmal was like no other with incredible, magical colors: pink and purple leaves, teal trunks, and silver branches. Abundant with enchanted fruit, there were often purple apples, rainbow colored peaches, and silver cherries on the same tree. The fruits grew year round and the people were never short of food, though they could not predict what colors the next season would bring.

"Aida, look!" Mara exclaimed. "Baby raccoons! Let's go play with them!"

Sure enough, at the river bank were three young raccoons splashing in the shallows, enjoying a morning bath. The marhilias glided over to the raccoons and gently splashed into their paws. As the raccoons dipped their busy little paws into the water, the girls jumped about, landing on their noses before bouncing back into the water, leaving the raccoons wet, but unharmed. Quick Current, Slow Current, back to the raccoons and repeat.

The young raccoons were delighted with their silvery playmates. They batted their paws into the air and tried in vain to capture the marhilias. One small raccoon got his paw over Aida. Thinking she was a small treat, he tried to pick her up. Aida laughed, fell into two parts, slipped out of the cub's paws and splashed back into the river.

"Mara! He tried to pick me up!" roared Aida.

"I saw! I saw it… he… you…" Mara was laughing so hard she didn't notice another raccoon had quietly put his small, gray muzzle in the river for a drink.

SLURP! The raccoon took a big gulp.

"Mara! Let one pick you up! Their paws are so…" Aida began describing her experience but then realized her friend was nowhere in sight.

"Mara? Mara? Where are you?" Aida dove down into the river.

Mara had to have gone for a deep dive. She was not on the river's surface or Aida would have seen or felt her. This was strange, she couldn't *sense* her friend. Aida dove deep and resurfaced without having found any sign of Mara.

"Mara? Mara!" she exclaimed.

Just then the baby raccoon coughed and sputtered. Stunned, he fell backwards onto the bank of the river. A water droplet on his chin started to giggle. Slowly, the droplet reformed into Mara.

"Mara!" Aida exclaimed in surprise, "What happened?"

Mara could hardly find the words, she was laughing so hard. "He..he…" Mara rolled back on the riverbank, "…he DRANK me!"

Aida looked at the astonished raccoon and then at her friend. Her sides started to shake. She snickered at the silly raccoon who was now chattering at them, scolding them. She bit her lip and looked at her friend for a moment. In seconds, both girls were in hysterics, laughing uncontrollably at the incident. They could feel the delight of all marhilias! *Everyone* – marhilias near and far, felt this funny incident and the river seemed to smile throughout the lands.

While Mara and Aida giggled over the incident with the thirsty raccoon, the river joyfully carried them along. The girls regained their composure and started small treks into the forest. Up this tree, along a teal branch, across a golden twig. Tip, touch. Tip, touch. They watered as they went.

Swish! Up another tree trunk- this one pink!

Skip, skip, skip right to the treetop, leaves of orange.

Drip, drop, drip, across greens.

"Mara," Aida asked, "What's your favorite tree?"

"Hmm," replied Mara, "that's tough! They are all so amazing. I love the ones with teal. No, purple! Purple ones. Ooh, but especially if they have those multicolor apples. I love the apples with the stripes. What's your favorite?"

"You're right, it is tough to say." Aida smiled back as she regarded the trees surrounding her. "I'd say my favorite is this one."

Aida bounded across the branches of a pink and yellow tree. It was very prominent, one of the biggest in the forest. It stood out proudly, showing off its sunny and soft hues. Fruits of all kinds were on this tree, but only in those two shades. Flamingo cherries, golden peaches, fuschia bananas. It was rare for a tree to parade only two colors- most trees in Cazmal showcased a fuller variety.

Mara regarded the big beauty and nodded. It *was* striking. Aida slid along a rosy branch then plopped back into the river.

5 The Plains of Zulta

The river widened and slowed to a gentle roll. The girls relaxed upon its current, traveling east towards the plains of Zulta. Golden prairies spanned across the horizon.

"It's so calm and quiet here," remarked Mara.

Aida thought about this for a moment, regarded her friend, and grinned.

Mara was such a tender sprite who was never upset or worried if things didn't go her way. She always knew just what to say. Aida watched the silvery lining of Mara's long hair flow as one with the river. Mara was especially delicate, even for a marhilia. Her fingers were smooth and small and her hands fit seamlessly into any water current. Aida often felt that her hands created small white caps or currents when she placed them in water, but not Mara. Mara was a gentle water sprite who could *ever* so silently blend in to any aquatic environment.

Her silvery eyes were soft and gentle, too. It was unusual for so much silver to be apparent in a marhilia's eyes, most were stark blue, the color of the river's deepest shade. Not Mara's. Aida had never seen anything like Mara's eyes and she loved that uniqueness about her friend.

"Are you ready to go through the wheat fields?" Mara interrupted her friend's thoughts.

"Yes, please!" Aida jumped up out of the river. She left a ripple where she had once been.

Mara laughed at her friend's sudden excitement and jumped out of the river to follow. The girls dodged and bobbed through the fields, leaving small traces of dew on each wheat sheaf. They bounded lightly from stalk to stalk, playing tag and chasing each other through golden blankets of corn. They were so light. They flew as they left dew droplets everywhere they touched down. In no time at all, the young marhilias had crossed a large number of fields.

"Mara! There's the river again! Let's go!" Aida spotted a tributary of the River Marcouera.

Marhilias can stay out of the river for extensive periods of time, sharing their water with the world of Terramara. It was what they were made to do. No matter where their journey took them, they always heard the river's gentle beckoning, sensed their watery sisters, and never felt alone.

6 The Caves of Decault

The afternoon sun sat lazily in the sky as the sprites floated out of Zulta. Here, the water was warmer and they enjoyed coasting along. Their next stop would be the Caves of Decault. Warm and cozy, filled with moss and gentle light, the caves were a favorite visiting place of humans and marhilias. Soft trickles of water flowed down the back of the ebony caves.

"It's a peaceful and relaxing place," they told each other as they slid from rock to rock, gently touching the few brave flowers that have beaten the odds in small cracks.

The rocks here in the south were a stark contrast to the white mountains. Their black surfaces collected heat from the sun and warmed the water that passed by. Medium sized pools filled with natural hot springs - heat from the earth and warmth from the sun - made them comfortable for everyone.

When the water's temperature changed, so did the marhilias. Their hues became a palette of warmer shades. Mara's spirit emitted a gentle pink.

"I like it when I'm pink and rosy," Mara smiled softly as she admired her shimmery shade. "It always makes me feel so cheerful."

Aida looked at her friend in the warmth and grinned. "You look happy when you're pink." She put her own hands in front of her face and snorted, "I just look like crazy, orange... fire!"

Mara laughed and regarded her friend. The orange shimmer was brighter here, Aida's prominent color. Mara soothed her friend. "You look warm. And important...

almost powerful. I like how bold you are in the caves."

Aida sighed. Mara would never understand. She transitioned through so many colors, all luxurious and beautiful. All soft and pretty. Aida, too, *had* other colors, but was always ruled by orange. (Orange was not her favorite. She wished for more blues or silver!)

Mara and Aida gently coasted around the caves, the water was shallow in the rocky formations. They took in the sights of the humans relaxing in the pools. The humans were fascinating. They wore tunics and maybrees all day and their skin *never* changed color. A *maybree* is a one piece jump suit that went from just above their knees to their shoulders. (The name comes from a combination of *maillot* and *breeches)*. Maybrees were suited for water, dried quickly and were easy to move around in. Tunics in blues, greens and purples were draped haphazardly on dry rocks along the side of the warm pools. The humans honored water by wearing the colors of the river in their daily clothing.

A woman in lavender softly splashed water onto her arms and it adjusted the direction that the girls were floating. They didn't mind. They floated with contentment and pleasure in the warmth. They were in no hurry to leave the black caves so they let the ebb and flow of the man-made waves send them where they pleased.

7 Sandy Bend

Eventually, they tired of the lazy caves and found a path back to Marcouera.

"I'm ready for the falls now." Mara smiled as she shifted back to an aquamarine shade.

"Me too," agreed Aida, who was now a softer, yellow shade.

As the two girls left the caves, the river widened and headed towards a huge bend. Luxurious banks of sand meandered from the bottom of the river up to the banks and beyond. Known as 'Sandy Bend' it was a natural gathering place for humans. Families met there to swim, play and relax.

Sandy Bend was a flurry of activity. Here, children splashed and played, had picnics, and visited with each other. Older children tread water and swam across the great width of the river.

The river here was reliable. Swimmers would cross the river and return easily. The people of Terramara were taught at a young age and were excellent swimmers. They spent their youth learning the currents and elements within Marcouera.

They would dive in, and start their crossing, all while the Slow Side moved them ever so slightly towards the Great Falls. In the final few strokes, right when they had *almost* crossed, the Quick Current would catch them. Whoosh! Swimmers could float quickly to their starting point but it took practice to find the right timing so the return-cross *and* the Slow Side could land you back to where you started. Learning these currents was a great challenge for many young humans.

Mara and Aida mixed in, unnoticed. They swam amongst serious-faced youth improving their skills and children splashing with glee. They danced off finger tips in motion and they slid down wet hair and noses. They were part of the water and enjoyed their fun games.

There were times the marhilias knew the humans could see them. It would only be for a fleeting moment. Their small size and super speed made it hard for humans to focus on... but every now and then a tiny connection would be made.

You could tell when the humans picked up on their game: Mara and Aida were rewarded with broad smiles and wide eyes filled with excitement. Much of the chatter from the children circled around this.

"I saw one!'

"Ooh! A marhilia just bounced off my nose..."

"Look! There, did you see?"

"I can't see any!"

"Are you sure?"

"Ah! Yes!"

"Hello!"

"Where?"

"I see one!"

"Look! Another one!"

And so, marhilias delighted in human activity at Sandy Bend. It was a pleasure to spend time at these crowded sandy beaches.

8 The Great Falls

Sandy Bend was adjacent to the Great Falls. The sand on the south bank faded to pebbles as you crossed the river and by the time you got to the other shore, huge boulders stacked on top of each other, slowly climbing up. A wide path was well worn for the first six feet of the falls.

There was a smooth, black platform where the path curved. Water gently trickled off this landing making it an easy starting point for beginning jumpers and divers.

Another fifteen feet up, the rocks got steeper and the path switchbacks twice. Here, the rocks showcased both white from Mardivina and black from Decalt. Ivory and ebony united as the rocks piled higher.

Water cascaded over this mid-point; rocks were slick, smoothed by the current over time. From this platform, older youth and adults jumped. This was the largest diving area and many humans gathered here. They relaxed, admired dives, and prepared to jump.

The top of the falls was another impressive twenty-feet up. The rock path narrowed substantially and only seasoned divers risked the climb. Single file only, the rocks transformed to the mountainous white. It was beautiful at the top. White rock shimmered as water deftly glided over it. As far as the eye could see, the river twinkled. When you stood at the height of the Great Falls, your heart beamed with peace and pride. It was an incredible sight to see. The forty-foot drop from here was formidable, but most humans in Terramara quickly rose to this challenge. Once you mastered the first two levels, it was most rewarding flying off the very top.

The falls cascaded into the deepest part of the river - so deep that it almost felt like a huge, bottomless lake. Here, far beyond the rocks and diving platforms was the heart of the river- a very special place for the marhilias. The heart of the river was what *called* to the water sprites; the Great Falls was a source of power that they all felt.

Thousands of marhilias could be found at the Great Falls at any time, day or night. They gathered there for comfort and peace. They connected with watery ripples. They dipped, danced, and dove constantly.

The Great Falls and Sandy Bend were located right at the edge of the palace's front yard. Terramara's citizens filled this spot daily; the castle opened to all people at all times. They were welcome to visit the gardens, courtyards and enjoy the beauty of the impressive white marble columns whenever they wished.

Soon, Aida and Mara would be at the base of the Waterfalls. There would be no need to climb rocks for the marhilias. They could simply flow *up* to join in on the diving fun!

9 Human Prince

Cyrus walked quietly through his father's gardens. He sighed as the reminder of his father's expectations weighed heavily on his heart: His father had been pushing for Cyrus to find a suitable partner for a while now.

It was not new to him. He had been preparing to run his father's kingdom for his entire life, and was familiar with the responsibilities that came along with it. It was his duty, and though Terramara did not have many protocols for the royal family, this one was expected.

He wished his mother was still here. She would know what to say. Though Cyrus and his father were close, his mother had a knack for lightening up any situation. She would understand what he was feeling- the conflict between wanting to please his father and wanting to follow his heart. Somehow, she would have been able to be on *both* sides at the same time- loving, understanding.

He sighed and kicked a loose pebble in front of him. His ebony hair was unruly and blew haphazardly in the breeze. His broad shoulders slumped under his royally tailored tunic. The crease between his brow made his gray-blue eyes appear angry, and his lip curled toward the right side of his face. He sighed again and carried on, alone in his thoughts.

He had tried, he really had! He felt he had given each and every one a fair chance, but there was always *something* missing. He was sure there had to be someone special- unique- for him. He couldn't explain it. He just knew what he had seen so far…and well, nothing felt right.

Cyrus sighed, frustrated with the argument he had

just had. He could still see the look of frustration and disappointment on his father's face as he refused yet another meeting. He disliked the rift with his father, for they were very close. This battle exhausted him. He knew his father wanted him to find a good match and wouldn't force him into marriage. He only wanted to encourage Cyrus, but truthfully, his efforts were heavy-handed, leaving Cryus overwhelmed and tired.

He walked on towards Sandy Bend at the end of the palace gardens. It was a popular place and easy to see why. Rich and lush, there was space to sprawl out on grasses. Trees lined the edge of the gardens, creating shade and competing with the marble columns that surrounded the palace grounds. The gardens eased into Sandy Bend.

Marhilias were constant sources of amusement and enjoyment. These little water sprites never ceased to amaze Cyrus with their constant energy and delight -- though half the time he wasn't sure if he saw marhilias or just splashes of water!

Mothers and their children waded in the shallows and splashed with the magical marhilias. Young children giggled as their faces were tickled by mist. Older children played games in the gentle rapids. They swam and dived, proud of their independence and open in their love of water. The River Maracoeura was warm, welcoming, and just as much part of the people's lives as it was home to the marhilias.

As Cyrus walked into the midst of his citizens, his scowl faded away. He was greeted with warm, loving smiles and waves from everyone. He returned all salutations, and for many people in Terramara, he was 'just another citizen.' A prince, to be sure, but the casual warmth he readily shared made people feel at ease around him. He was one of them.

In fact, the only difference you could actually see between the prince and the people of Terramara was the silver embroidery along his tunic. The edges of his cuffs and the hems at his knees were special. Delicate designs of water and waves adorned the prince's clothing. It was fine work, small and intricate. In Terramara, this was enough to distinguish the royals. (Not that anyone needed telling. The prince knew all his citizens by name, and they called him Cyrus, which he insisted upon.)

His spirits lifted with friendly chit chat as he adjusted his meandering pace to a brisk walk, heading towards the falls. He was ready to shake off his gloom and dive! Diving always took his mind off his troubles.

10 The Top of the Falls

From the mid-section of the falls, young adults challenged one another to dive to the bottom, racing each other and the unbeatable marhilias.

"Cyrus!" a voice yelled from the mid-shelf of the cliffs. "Come! Join us!"

Cyrus recognized his longtime friend, Johatt. Wildly waving and smiling, Johatt motioned for his friend to climb up.

Cyrus smiled. He stripped his blue tunic off and hung it on a branch. Tunics in Terramara had mid- length sleeves, covered the shoulders and cinched around the waist with a belt. Though it was seldom cold in Terramara, if needed, the tunics could be opened and used as a wrap.

Cyrus climbed the rock face with ease in his aquamarine maybree. A dozen or so citizens were along the rocky platform, waving at friends below and above, as they contemplated their best launch spot. They smiled warmly as the prince came into view.

"Cyrus, you climb like an old man! The years are not kind... perhaps you had better choose a wife before you lose your looks too," Johatt roared, laughing at his own joke. He knew of Cyrus's difficulties but his friendly nature and love made Cyrus smile. His friend meant no harm.

It was well known that the king was anxious for a match to happen. Some of the people flashed Cyrus a sympathetic glance. They wanted their prince to be happy.

"Yes, but... it's not easy..." Cyrus trickled off, aware

of the crowd.

"Well," Johatt interrupted, "I had no troubles and I have fans as well!"

He gestured to the group of youth down below, keenly watching the jumpers dive. Some had just finished their own dives and were excited to watch others take the plunge. Cheers of approval rang out whenever someone launched.

"Yes. Yes. Most of them are here to see me. It's true," Johatt bragged with a joking smile.

"Ha!" a young woman interrupted. "If he spent half the time actually diving instead of flexing his muscles at the top of the mountain, we might find something of interest to see!"

Lila had just climbed up the rock side in her teal suit and joined in the conversation. An avid fan of the falls and diving herself, she added coyly, "Perhaps, Johatt, my dear, you would make better use of the water down in the shallows, where you can be properly adored- by yourself!"

At that, many people at the cliff top chuckled, including Johatt himself. The reflective power of the water in the shallows made it mirror smooth.

"I guess I have to prove you wrong, Lila!" Johatt winked at Cyrus as he launched himself off the rocks. His body streamlined with the falls and his navy colors blurred with the cascade.

Cyrus regarded Lila as she watched Johatt's jump in admiration. It was well known that Johatt and Lila were one of the best-liked couples in Terramara. Strong, outgoing, and easy to get along with, it was plain to see why they were a good match.

Cyrus's train of thought was interrupted as Lila let

out a loud whoop and followed her husband off the cliff. Streamlined, she broke smoothly into the water alongside Johatt. They surfaced together and laughed in the mix of mist and marhilias below.

"Cyrus! Come on! We're waiting!" they splashed one another as the river carried them slowly to shore.

11 Cyrus's Dive

Briefly regarding the couple he adored, Cyrus grinned, and then returned his attention to the warm waters before him. Today, he needed to jump from the top shelf. He turned to face the white rock and began to ascend. It didn't take him long. In his form-fitted maybree, moving was quick. The narrow path of rock was easy enough with his agility. Standing on the top, he looked down and saw that his friends had made it to the shallows. They beckoned to him with waves and yelling.

With one powerful stride he moved forward and plummeted toward the water below. His arms were overhead, tight in front of his face and he raced the falls as they cascaded down. He sliced the river's surface and felt his body slow with the weight of the water all around. It was warm and welcoming.

Cyrus opened his eyes and saw the rocks of the river not far below. Determined to touch the deep bottom before resurfacing, he kicked his legs and engaged his arms in a powerful front stroke.

The river was extremely deep here, not many could make it to the bottom, even with the force of a good dive. But Cyrus was determined. Three more strong pulls advanced him to the river's bottom. Cyrus let his hands sink into the black pebbles, lowered his legs, preparing to lunge to the surface, glanced upward toward the light, then paused.

Something caught his eye.

He squinted in the water to see what was before him.

Shimmering and fluid, he could vaguely make out a shape.

A woman?

No, there was no real body before him.

What was it?

It appeared to be the same size as Cyrus yet he couldn't be sure.

His need for air was drawing near and just before Cyrus squatted once more to propel to the surface, his eyes met the most incredible sight he had ever seen in his life.

Stunned silver eyes held Cyrus's gaze.

Suddenly, his lungs no longer hurt, it was as though his need for air disappeared and he was connected with these mysterious eyes. Cyrus regarded the figure more closely; it was indeed a beautiful woman...yet, not a woman.

There was something strange about her. She was silver, or maybe blue. He reached for her and saw his own flesh colored hand.

She reminded Cyrus of a marhilia, but surely couldn't be, for they were the size of a dew drop and before him floated a translucent woman of similar size to him!

How could this be?

What *was* he seeing?

And why could he not look away?

The watery figure smiled at Cyrus, her eyes softening. She seemed as amazed as Cyrus at the interaction between them, as though she had never seen a human before. Cyrus knew he had never seen anything like her before. She was exquisite.

Cyrus reached out to touch her hand but it went right through hers. It was as if she was made of water. Cyrus felt as though time had stopped. He could scarcely draw himself away from her gaze.

The figure reached out her hands. This time, their fingers touched in a slippery grasp that felt soft and warm. They didn't feel like human hands and Cyrus marveled at their softness.

Time passed as they hovered in the deeps together. Their eyes were locked onto one another with curiosity and awe. An underwater current interrupted the spell and the figure guided him to the surface.

Cyrus did not wish their meeting to end, but was compelled to float upwards with her. Finally he emerged, spluttering and coughing. Twisting and turning, he searched for the figure he had just been entranced with but she was nowhere to be seen.

There was only concerned onlookers and water.

12 Concern

"Cyrus! Cyrus! Are you okay?" Johatt swam over to his friend and guided him to the bank of the river.

Lila helped haul Cyrus onto the bank. Concerned citizens gathered around and a quiet murmur surrounded Cyrus who could not draw his eyes away from the water.

"Cyrus," Lila gently shook him, "Are you okay? You were under the river for a long time."

"What were you doing?" demanded Johatt, worry pounding through his voice. "What happened to you? Are you okay?"

Cyrus slowly surfaced back to reality, forcing himself to look away from the water. He shook his head. Worried faces surrounded him.

"Cyrus?' Lila softly whispered, "Are you okay?"

Cyrus blinked and nodded mutely.

"Let's get him back to the palace," Johatt said, taking charge. "He'll be fine. I think he just needs a moment."

Johatt hauled Cyrus to his feet in one strong fluid motion. Cyrus's legs felt like jelly beneath him and he was surprised by how much he depended on his friend's strength to stand. He smiled weakly at Johatt and allowed Lila to weasel herself under his other arm.

"He'll be fine, everyone," Johatt told the concerned crowd, "Just trying to keep up with me, I'm sure!"

Lila raised an eyebrow and gave a knowing look to Johatt. She knew his worry for his friend was much fiercer than he was letting on. Still, he felt he needed to reassure others around him. Typical Johatt. A few people chuckled at Johatt's comment, but there was nervousness in their laughter. This was, after all, not just any man, but their beloved prince.

"A little space, please," Lila beseeched.

The crowd dispersed, allowing the couple to lead Cyrus away from the river.

"I'm fine,' Cyrus whispered, "Really... I ..."

His words were interrupted with a chesty cough.

"Steady, my friend," Johatt softly directed, "Lila and I will see you home now. And not another word. There's a lot of worried people here and we don't want to alarm anyone."

Cyrus looked into Johatt's eyes and saw the concern his friend had for him. Johatt knew Cyrus was an excellent swimmer, one of the best in all Terramara. Surely there wasn't cause for this much fuss.

Or was there?

How long had Cyrus been in the river?

13 Mara

Mara surfaced from the river on the far bank immediately looking for the man she had just seen. Her whole being was flushed with a strange emotion. It was unlike any sensation she had ever known.

Mara was vibrating.

She could feel the river's enchantment, the strength of every marhilia, but there was something more, something bigger. They all felt it, something magical, yet it was only Mara who'd connected with a human.

How was this possible?

What had just happened?

She had seen this human before, as she had countless other humans, but now his name came back to her.

Cyrus.

She had never maintained contact with one human for *so long*.

She had never shared any deep water experience with a human before.

This was so…so … *unusual*.

How could he withstand the water so long?

And how was it that he appeared to be *her size*?

She regarded the humans on the river banks and once again felt their size overpower her. She was small and they were large.

Her fingertips were emblazoned with hot water as she searched the riverbanks.

Where was he?

Was he okay?

She saw the crowd of people on the banks and realized their mood had shifted. They were concerned about something. Concerned about him. So, it wasn't just her imagination. He *had* been underwater with her that whole time.

But the question was: did he feel what she felt?

Mara flitted and flipped on the surface of the water.

Vibrant colors were left behind where her flaming fingertips trickled along.

She had to find answers.

Did he know what just happened?

Did he feel the same?

Could he explain it?

She was determined to find out.

14 Return to the Palace

"Johatt. Lila, please. I'm fine," Cyrus protested wearily.

"Cyrus. You were missing a long time. We're just relieved you're okay now," Lila spoke.

Cyrus blinked at her. There was no point quarreling with Johatt and Lila.

He had to admit he *was* feeling a bit weak. Besides, Cyrus was too distracted to argue. He plodded along, quietly listening to Johatt lecturing on his left while a concerned Lila supported him on his right.

"Cyrus, honestly, what were you doing down there? What happened? We couldn't see you from the surface." Johatt's worry subsided into anger.

"Johatt, come on." Cyrus rolled his eyes. "There's nothing to worry about."

They arrived at the palace and were greeted by many concerned citizens crowded between the white marble columns. They were giving the trio space. Word had traveled fast about Cyrus's mishap.

By now, Cyrus's legs were supporting his weight and he could strongly project his voice.

"Please," Cyrus addressed the onlookers. "There's nothing to worry about. Thank you for your concern, but there's no need. I'm fine." He dismissively and casually waved his hand in the air.

People smiled warmly, as their kind and gentle prince alleviated their concerns. A small murmur went through the crowd. Many at the palace thought that the episode had been exaggerated by those on the banks. Concern for someone who had gone under water was normal, but surely no concern would ever be needed for Cyrus.

Cyrus carried himself up the white marble stairs, Johatt and Lila closely in check. They were met by the king, Anzoil, who had also heard the news.

The king turned and walked alongside his son. Openly relieved that Cyrus was okay, he put his arm around his son's shoulders and gave him a strong squeeze. Cyrus paused, patted his father's hand, and smiled at him. His father had always openly shown his love.

Cyrus led the crew into the royal library and sat down. He smiled.

"How can you just sit there and smile?" Johatt demanded. "We were really worried!"

"Johatt, I can see that. I can feel how much *every* citizen was concerned for my well-being and I can see you and Lila have been shaken by what has just happened. "But," Cyrus tried to calm his friend, "I assure you I am fine."

"Cyrus," Lila placed her hand on Cyrus's arm quietly. "What did happen today? We thought… I mean.. you were under there a *long* time… *too* long..."

Lila trailed off and looked sideways at Johatt.

Johatt continued, "Cyrus, it *was* too long. It was simply too long. Even for *you.* It is impossible to stay underwater that long. You shouldn't have been able to swim up alone after all that time, and there's no way you could be *just fine.*"

Cyrus looked at his father, Lila, then Johatt and sighed inwardly. His two best friends, he never had any secrets from them. He could confide in them without doubting their alliance. He could always rely on their sound counsel and care. They were not there to judge him, only to listen and help, always.

And the king, his own father. They had always been close, their bond only stronger after his mother had passed. It was just the two of them now and his father also had his full confidence.

And here he was on the day the most profound and wonderful experience happened to him and he was not sure how to tell them.

"Something did happen to me," Cyrus began, "but it's a little difficult to explain. Well, it's difficult to understand as well."

And Cyrus began to tell them about the mysterious figure he had seen beneath the water, about the silver eyes, and the warmth he felt while he was near her. Mouths agape, they listened silently as they tried to make sense of Cyrus's story.

15 Aida's Discovery

"Mara!" A voice interrupted her search. "Mara!"

Mara started. She shook herself and found the voice that was calling her. She saw Aida with an excited look, diving in and out of the wake on her way to Mara, fast.

Aida exclaimed, "WHAT just happened? Did you feel that? Something rippled in the river. Something powerful. We all felt it. It's like Marcouera's spirit … well.. I don't know. We don't know… everyone is buzzing!"

Aida continued, "I didn't see you, I thought you were still beside me but once the energy started to shift in the river, I couldn't move. Could you?"

"No…," Mara was distant, "I was still… under … the falls….well, down the river a bit…."

"What? You weren't in the mist? I know, I couldn't feel you for a moment. I could feel everyone, except you. That is odd, too! I wonder what it means." Aida was talking and splashing her way up the falls again, buzzing amongst other marhilias who had also felt the surge.

"Aida, wait! I want to tell you something…." Mara began. But she didn't know where to begin. Why did she have a *single* experience? Why didn't Aida feel what Mara had felt? This was the first time she felt *individual*. It was new. And strange. And she didn't know what it meant.

Her thoughts were interrupted by a chattering Aida. "Mara, come on! Get up here!" Aida was at the top of the falls and ready to release.

Mara grinned as she watched her friend's face,

full of sheer joy, letting the falls encapsulate her as she flowed over the edge.

Mara glanced once more at the shore, but not finding the face she longed to see, she decided to join her friend at the falls.

16 Cyrus's Thoughts

Cyrus went to his room to rest. He could not get the figure out of his mind. It was so odd. She was not human! But how could she be a marhilic?

He had seen millions of marhilias. His whole life he had been taught their ways and was happily surrounded by them. They were in the river, the rain, his bath, and the water everywhere. They were water fairies and they were all the same to him.

But not *this one*.

There was something different about this one.

But what? Why did he feel differently now? What had happened in the River Marcouera just then? Surely they had just shared a moment together and he was not alone in his experience. She felt it too. He just knew it. He saw it in her eyes. He had to see her again. But how?

He did not know her name. He did not even know if marhilias were entirely separate from one another.

How could this be?

Was he in love?

And if so, was it with one marhilia… or all of them?

17 Connection

Cyrus. Mara said his name over and over again. His name revolved in her mind until it began to flow like water and felt like a part of her. Somehow Cyrus's spirit had flowed into hers- like another marhilia's. But he was human! Only the river's spirit could touch a marhilia.

And yet, here it was. A connection.

A feeling of kindness. No, no, not kindness...this was more than kindness...what was she feeling? She did not know a word for it, but she knew he had felt it too.

Mara had not seen him since she left the falls that day. But she knew what she must do. She went to Aida first to tell her friend.

"What do you mean? You share a spirit? What kind of spirit? He does not have a *water* spirit. And a human cannot stay in the water *that* long. At least not under the water. Mara, what are you talking about?" Aida fired off rapid questions.

"I know it sounds strange, I'm still trying to understand it. But I know he felt it too. You should have seen his face. I feel connected to him now. It's different than it is with you, the others, the river..." Mara paused, searching for more words to make Aida understand. "With Marcouera, we all feel each other's presence, we blend together and feel like we are one. We know which areas of Terramara are being watered, even if we ourselves are not there. We can sense each other, even from great distances. The connection I feel with him..." she paused in thought. "... it's different from anything I've ever experienced before."

Aida furrowed her brow in disbelief. "Really? Can

that happen? Can a human feel a water spirit? How come I didn't feel him? *No* other marhilia felt it. How come *you* are alone in this?'

"I don't know," Mara whispered. "It's so weird that you cannot feel what I feel right now. I wish I had more words to... to...explain it better."

It was difficult for Mara. She realized she was alone in this, nobody else had felt what she did. She knew that now. It was a heavy feeling, but she still wanted to try to help Aida understand.

Mara looked at her friend, "I do know one thing. He and I have are connected now- somehow. Something has happened to me. I'm different now."

Aida was speechless, but only for a moment.

"This is outrageous! I don't believe it. What do you mean 'you're different now?' You are a marhilia! You are one with us. Why does no one else feel this? I don't. Nothing happened to me. Mara, why are you saying this?"

"Aida, his spirit calls me," Mara explained. "Cyrus and I are connected now. It is different than what I'm used to but stronger than anything I have ever known."

"Cyrus? Calls you? What do you mean? Mara. Enough. I don't understand!" Aida's eyes flickered anger.

She flitted away from Mara, hurt and confused.

Mara sighed. How could she explain this to her friend when she did not fully understand it herself?

"Aida?" Mara whispered, "He calls to me inside my heart. Like Marcouera."

"Like Marcouera? How is that possible? Mara, please..." Aida stopped and faced her friend.

"I hear them *both* now. The call from Marcouera and

another calling- it's Cyrus's spirit. He calls me to him. He doesn't even know it, not in the way that I know. But I do. I am used to being called. Marcouera has called me my entire life and I know this type of calling." Mara looked upon her friend. "It is a connection that I cannot ignore."

Aida stopped herself from protesting and looked into her friend's silver eyes. Trying to understand, she smiled weakly.

"It's okay. Don't worry, Aida," Mara said, "I will be alright."

"But...but... what does this mean?"Aida's voice was barely audible.

With new certainty, Mara declared, "The river is guiding me now. I know what I must do. Can you hear it? Can you feel the heart?"

Aida said nothing, and with her shoulders slumped she lowered her eyes. Finally, she spoke. "Yes, I can feel it. You know I can. We all feel it now- the heart of the river is calling us all. It's been a long time since we were summoned that deep. I feel Marcouera's spirit, a call that we have not felt in thousands of years. Now I feel it. I feel that something ....*change*... is coming. Yes, yes, I feel it. But it can't be YOU! You are not the change that is coming! It must be something else."

"Aida," Mara lifted her friend's face and looked gently into her eyes. "I don't know why this is becoming clearer to me. I am starting, even now, to feel separate from you and the others. I know that I am the only one who hears two voices at this moment. I cannot ignore the river, and I cannot ignore Cryus. Our destinies are now linked. We will find out what is next together. Marcouera will make everything known tonight. We will gather in the heart of the river tonight."

Aida danced one last water dance in Marcouera with her friend. They laughed and splashed and swam. They painted the flowers in the meadow with dew and touched the trees sleeping in the night. They flowed in the river, letting the water roll quietly over them. Silent waves were tears on the banks as Aida and Mara shared their last night together.

"Come with me to see him," Mara whispered. She knew something important was about to happen. But what? She would listen to her spirit and the river; they would guide her tonight.

Aida straightened up. The river was alive within her and bade her to go with her friend. She nodded and they flitted towards the palace.

18 The Meeting

As they bounded across the gardens, Aida smiled at her friend. She could not recall the human called Cyrus. She was curious to see who he was and to see if he really was as unique as Mara claimed.

And though she could not feel her friend's joy for the same reason, she was happy for her, for the river had whispered the news: *Mara had been chosen and change was coming.*

"Mara, I have to admit, I'm excited to see who you have this new connection with. To be honest, I never pay attention to *this* human or *that* human, they are just so big! I don't spend much time wondering about them at all."

They arrived at the palace steps and bounded in. It was a bit odd, there was no need for marhilias to enter the palace, as they went where greenery was and here was only white marble. Small drops of water were left in their wake and they trickled along the grand entrance.

Before long, they saw the prince, reading. They raced over and climbed up a desk. Cyrus sighed and looked up from his book. *Ancient History of Elementia* sat open on his lap. Curiously, he regarded the floor. A trail of water? What was this? His eyes followed the stream, along the tile, to the desk. Up, to the looking glass that sat beside scrolls he had been reviewing.

Silently the marhilias watched him in mutual fascination.

Cyrus reached forward and ran his finger through a pool of water on the desk's corner. Quickly, he lifted his hand and inspected it. He silently wondered about the marhilia he saw under the falls.

Oh, how he could not free his mind from her! How she had impressed upon his entire being. He loved her. He was sure. Would he ever see her again though? What was wrong with him? He hoped the ancient stories could shed some light on what was happening.

He sighed again and thought of returning to the falls tomorrow. He would go every day until eternity to see this marhilia again. Nothing made sense. He hoped he would find answers at the river.

Mara and Aida watched in silence. Aida liked him. She liked the way he gently stirred the water and the soft smile upon his face. Gently, she pushed her friend forward.

Mara slid down the mirror, sparkling. It caught the prince's eye. He squinted and leaned in toward the droplet. He placed his finger at the end of the stream and in the next moment, a smiling Mara emerged on his fingertip.

"It's you!" Cyrus gasped and leaned in close.

Mara smiled, "Yes."

"And you can talk! I mean, we can talk. I have never talked to a water sprite before. I mean, marhilia." Cyrus vibrated with excitement. What luck that she would appear here at his desk!

And then, what bad luck to see that she *was* just a water sprite. What was wrong with him? Moments ago, he was convincing himself that he loved her and now, here she was... almost a simple drop of water.

Well, not that simple...after all, she *was* talking to him. He lifted his hand so that his soft gray eyes were at the same level as hers.

Their eyes met and they both felt the connection

they felt in the river. Despite size and difference a link had been made. They regarded one another in silence, both wondering the same things. So many unanswered questions.

Aida trickled forward to the edge of the mirror.

"So *you* are the human who can *live* underwater," Aida interrupted.

Cyrus looked up with a start at the water sprite on his mirror. He glanced around for others. Mara smiled at his awareness.

"It's only the two of us," Aida stated. "Cyrus. Is that your name?"

"Yes," Cyrus answered, "that's correct. And who, who are you? And why is this the first time I have ever spoken to a water sprite before!? I mean, it's incredible, but also weird. Am I the only one who finds this strange?"

Aida began to explain, "Yes, it *is* strange. Certainly nothing like this has ever happened to us in the river before. I am Aida and this is Mara."

"Mara." Her name flowed from his lips for the first time. "Hello, Mara."

Her tiny being glimmered, "Hello Cyrus."

Oddly, he wanted to know more about her name. As if reading his mind, Aida continued.

"Mara is a very strong name," she told him proudly, "Mara is from the first line of Marhilias. That means she was one of the very first to be created when Marcouera died."

"Marcouera. *Queen* Marcouera," Cyrus confirmed and he laid his hand on the book he had been reading, "She is at the heart of the River. Marcouera. The river was named after her when she saved Terramara from the fires."

"Yes," Aida answered, pleased that Cyrus knew. "When she sacrificed herself to ensure Terramara's survival she became the river. We are very glad to hear your knowledge."

"*We*?" questioned Cyrus.

"Yes, we are all connected, every water sprite. We feel and know what everyone feels in the river. Until now. Mara has felt something different, something only she experienced. Something with you."

"Connected? This is all so incredible. And yes, yes, I felt something different in the river, too. Something powerful. I *was* underwater for longer than a human can withstand and yet I am fine now." Cyrus was excited but then his brow furrowed.

"I can't understand why you are still so small."

He looked at Mara. He tilted his head to see the tiny bead.

"Cyrus," Mara spoke again. "It's the same for me. I know you experienced what I did in the river. An ancient magic surrounded us so that we could connect. That is what made us appear the same size. You thought *I* was big, but I thought *you* were small. Whatever it really was, we were the same size in that moment. That magic is what allowed you to stay underwater without dying. I don't really know what is next, but Marcouera's magic is guiding me now. She has been weak, slowly fading over these last hundreds of years. And soon, she will perish. We will both have answers soon. I promise."

Cyrus solemnly nodded, "I believe we are part of each other's destinies now."

Mara smiled knowingly. She was about to continue when suddenly, both sprites jolted towards the river.

The call was strong and they needed to go. *Now!*

Heeding the river's voice, the two marhilias slipped off the desk and slid towards the marble entrance.

"Wait!' Cyrus called, "Where are you going? What does this mean? When will I see you again?"

"We must go now," Aida said firmly. "We are being called."

"It will all make sense in time." Mara smiled. "The river is calling to us and we must go."

And with that, they were gone in a blink.

"Am I crazy?" Cyrus wondered. "Did I just talk to marhilias?" He looked around, wondering about this experience. He wasted no more time pondering the events alone. He went to find the king.

19 Still Waters

Every marhilia answered the call from Marcouera. They swam and dove to the river's heart, congregating as quickly as possible, moving in unison. The river held its breath leaving the outside world still and silent.

Marcouera had been fading, slowly seeping away despite her brave effort to send water sprites into the world. She could no longer sustain them. The connective power between the river, sprites, and world above was slipping away like water through fingertips. The world as they knew it would soon be no more.

The marhilias, the remaining pieces of Marcouera, arrived in its depths. An anticipation filled the air as the water sprites circled together far beneath the glass-like surface.

Mara and Aida were both directed by the power in the river to the center of the meeting. The marhilias whisked together creating one large cyclone around them. They were in awe of the power they could feel encompassing them. Wide-eyed, the girls observed the massive twister surrounding them. They felt loved and protected.

In the next moment the gentle cyclone moved to a figure-eight shape, creating two identical swirls, side by side. Mara at the center of one, Aida in the other. They were not afraid. The sparkling and glimmering was dreamlike. The swell of water began to link the rest of the marhilias together. Water drove into their beings and both Mara and Aida grew in size.

Mara was full of water and sparkle and grew to the size of her human form. Her figure twinkled in the river's heart and her feelings for Cyrus were released for all to experience.

A tingle of excitement rippled through the watery depths as the whole river felt the special connection with a human. It was a new and unique sensation. Mara smiled inwardly at the feeling and beamed. Now, every marhilia would know it was true. Aida shot her a grin.

Aida was also a large watery figure but her shape was different. Many marhilias joined together to create her form and you could see tiny, blue lines glowing between each droplet. She resembled Marcouera, an enchantress in a blue robe, and when Aida spoke it was a watery choir unifying thousands of small voices.

"Our destiny is changing. Long ago, before Marcouera was a river, she was our ruling Goddess. Her sacrifice saved this world and we have been the ones supporting its life and growth. Our gift was one of peace and water."

Mara, floating in the midst of spinning sprites, listened carefully to the enchantress' words.

The voice of the many continued. "The time has come for the world to take care of itself. We have all felt the water slowly changing and it is losing its power. Soon, we will all be gone. The magic of the river will fade. Terramara can go on but humans must take care of it. We must teach them the ways of the marhilias. The river will still run in this land but without magic."

Mara listened intently. A barrage of prophecies surrounded her from all sides in the water. It was hard to know where to look. She turned within the current to focus on the voices:

"The water will come from rains, beginning in the Mardivina mountains."

"The river will flow in one direction."

"The columns are the answer."

"You must teach them."

"Every plant needs you, Mara."

"Cyrus is your partner. You will know what to do together."

"Tend to the desert."

The words came faster now and were a blur to Mara. As the words continued to surround her, she felt herself being taken away from the heart of the river, toward the surface and Sandy Bend. She saw the figure of Aida fading in her sights.

"The columns!"

"The marhilias."

"Columns. Water. Teach. Cyrus. Desert."

Mara's transformation used much of the final strength from the river's heart. As Mara was transported toward her new life, still part marhilia, not quite human, she felt the impact of the change. With a mix of great sadness and joy, she knew there were only hundreds of marhilias left and their time was limited. Even still, joy was in her heart, a new human heart, which kept beating as she moved toward her future.

With one final swirl, Marcouera dissolved into soft, blue waves. The collective voice was silent. Aida and a small handful of marhilias hovered where there were once millions of sprites.

In the distance, they could see the blue light carrying Mara to shore. They gravitated together and watched Mara finally leave the water in solemn silence.

As the figure of Mara hovered between the river and the land, waiting for the final magic, the marhilias' next act was to send their voice and message to the prince.

This time, the river would go to Cyrus.

Silently, the marhilias swirled together once more, into the shape of Marcouera with Aida at the helm, floating up out of the river as one, towards the palace.

20 The Library

Cyrus told his father about the visit with vibrant enthusiasm. The king was equally excited. Together, they rapidly scanned the library. White marble columns and archways stood proudly, their shelves stuffed with books and scrolls, teeming with untapped knowledge.

Where was the prophecy about the river and the marhilia with silver eyes? The one that spoke of a transformation using the ancient blue crystals? They had both read it, known it was part of their history, but for the event to be now, in their lifetime... it was inconceivable!

Anzoil regarded his son and admired his gray eyes. He listened as Cyrus described Mara's silver eyes. The king felt a surge of excitement for his son and he continued searching. Parchments, books, and scrolls covered the table. They scanned for information about ancient prophecies. Anzoil had his hands on one scroll in particular: one that foretold of a transformation and the enchantments that were destined to follow.

This scroll had been written shortly after Marcouera's sacrifice and it had been carefully preserved for centuries in the royal library. He couldn't have imagined that this grand event would happen in his lifetime. His son!

"How are you feeling?" The king tilted his head towards Cyrus.

"Excited. Nervous. I'm not sure," Cyrus told him, grinning as he tried to explain. "I feel like the anticipation of what's next is going to burst from within me. When I connected with Mara, when we spoke today... I mean we *talked*... it was like I didn't even notice she was a small sprite. It just felt like a normal conversation."

The king nodded, listening and encouraging his son to go on.

"I mean, I noticed her sitting on my fingertip so, of course, I saw how small she was... but, *inside*- inside, it didn't feel odd. It just felt like I was talking with a friend I've always had. It was weird and wonderful to talk to a marhilia, but it also felt so normal."

"That's incredible," remarked his father, "just incredible."

Cyrus prattled on. "My head is just swimming with what's next. I know something is coming, but I just can't piece the puzzle together in my mind. I wonder if Mara will return tonight? Or tomorrow? When will we meet again?"

The king watched his son's whirlwind of emotions. He tried to consider what it was like and he wondered if he would ever get the chance to talk with a marhilia himself.

21 The Visit

As the men bustled around the library, scouring over papers and pages, a soft light entered the palace. A wisp of blue swished into the library above them. Slowly, they looked up. Silently, the king and his son came together, in awe. A line of twinkly water formed a halo around them. It cascaded down and surrounded them in a gentle watery circle. They stood, encompassed by liquid, but neither man got wet. The water flowed continuously around them without touching the ground.

A soft voice filled the room, "Cyrus it is time. Tonight. Go to the river. Mara is waiting. Bring a robe, a maybree, and tunic. Tonight. Go to the river. Bring the blue enchanted crystals. Tonight."

The watery voice hovered up over their heads once again, then silently floated out the palace entrance. They watched it circle the columns and return to the river.

After a moment, Cyrus turned to his father with a grin. The blue crystals! Anzoil smiled to himself, then aloud he said, "The crystals. Come with me!"

Cyrus grinned and followed his father, scroll still in hand, to the south gardens.

22 Blue Crystals

They raced down the marble stairs and strode over to the four white columns. Unlike the other columns that surrounded the palace, these four stood only three feet tall. They were delicately carved from top to bottom with images of water sprites, rivers and rocks.

"Now what do we do?" asked Cryus.

It was known by all the citizens of Terramara that the ancient blue crystals were within these particular columns. The columns had been here for as long as Terramara had existed. The only thing the royal pair didn't know was how to get the crystals out. Men had tried in the past but the strong marble was formidable. Unbreakable, in fact. Hundreds of years had passed and still the legend of the blue crystals lived on, safely guarded by these four.

"They're wet," remarked Cyrus once he got closer to the columns.

"Remarkable," noted the king. His eyes darted around, searching.

Both men wondered the same thing: Were the marhilias here? They weren't entirely sure who their enchanted message had come from.

They ran their hands along the columns, seeking a way in, inspecting and hoping.

Cyrus searched the first, then the second. When he laid his hands on the third beam, Anzoil stood back. The column glowed. Water slipped upwards and softly covered Cyrus's hands. A soft light emanated around him.

The king circled around, watching this moment in awe. He could sense the power that was here now and he could see that his son was part of it.

Cyrus looked at his hands in amazement, saw the watery magic and knelt. He held tight to the column and closed his eyes. Water from all four columns was drawn into his hands now. Tiny rainbows of water leapt towards the prince. Cyrus was not getting wet, the water seemed to become one with him, absorbing into his hands.

In moments, the water stopped, the columns were dry and Cyrus was still. Anzoil held his breath as he concentrated on his son's face, unsure of what would happen next.

When Cyrus opened his eyes, the king gasped.

Silver. His son's eyes were sparkling and silver.

Cyrus was concentrating on the column. He squinted, inspected the columns and realized they were slowly moving. It was magic. The marble carvings came alive in his very hands. The stone river *flowed* where water was carved, creating small openings in each column.

After a moment, the white marble was still again. Cyrus let his hands fall to his side and stood. He tilted his head and saw what he was meant to find: A sparkling blue crystal, hovering inside the white beam. It appeared to be floating within the center. Cyrus reached for it then took a step back.

The crystal lay in the palm of his hand, glowing and glittering.

Cyrus grinned at his father, then one by one, went to each column and gently picked out the crystal. When all four were collected, he went to his father's side.

"Aren't they beautiful?" Cyrus held them out in his palm.

"Yes," he agreed, "they are incredible."

Each crystal was a varying shade of blue: teal,

sapphire, royal, and navy. They twinkled with life in Cyrus's hand. The crystals were delicate, long and slender, each one the size of a small finger. They resembled the marble columns, sleek and smooth.

Side by side, as they admired the crystals, the king noticed his son's eyes. They were gray again but seemed different somehow. Small silver flecks sparkled within them.

"I must go." Cyrus turned and bounded towards the castle to complete his tasks.

His father was fast on Cyrus's heels, "Wait! There is something I must give you."

They rushed through the palace together then the king watched his son sprint out of sight, then he returned back to the newly opened columns.

He inspected the marble structures. How firm those carvings were once again! They were rock solid. If he had not seen this magic with his own eyes, it would be hard to believe.

And something else he did not expect: the columns were hollow! Entirely hollow. The crystals had been floating in their magical centers.

'Incredible,' he murmured and he slipped his hand inside to be sure.

23 To The River

As Cyrus reached the river bank, water shot up and hovered in front of him. Puzzled, he paused and regarded the large watery pool in front of him. He did not know what he was witnessing, but felt strangely calm and wasn't surprised when the voice came from within.

"Cyrus, hear me. You are a human *with* a water spirit. You have a human spirit too, but the water within you means you are special. You are the one who will help Mara keep the world alive. Soon, Mara will have a human spirit and you will both be connected twice over."

Just above the river, the outline of a human shape glowed silver with shimmering light. Water swirled around the figure. The rivers, streams, and lakes in the land sat silent and still except here. The energy of all the water in Terramara was here and Mara's change was almost complete. It would be unstoppable now.

Cyrus searched the swirling figure of water, hoping to see Mara's face. Hoping to feel that connection once more. He wistfully leaned forward.

Slowly, the voice continued. "Your human connection with Mara will begin once the river releases her. Cyrus, the final task is to return the enchanted crystals to the river."

The watery figure changed, transformed to Mara. Silently, Cyrus stretched out his fingers and met her sleek touch.

Time stood still as the couple's eyes locked; flickering the same silvery shade. Only their fingers touched as he stood on the bank and she was still embraced entirely by water, floating in the air in front of him, half human, half water.

"The crystals must be presented to the four corners of the river. They will complete the transformation. When the last crystal finds its home, the river's flow will adjust, the heart of the river will fade and Mara will be human."

Cyrus smiled and clenched the crystals tightly. He placed the beautiful blue clothing he had brought for human Mara on the shore and started down the river on a paddle board.

Briskly, surely, he made his way. The moonlight shimmered on the river and he thought how odd it was that the river was so still. Especially on the mountain! Despite the downward flow the water was completely still and silent. There was no rushing, no current and no marhilias. It was frozen in time.

He dipped his finger into the river and was surprised to see no ripple, no life, no change at all. It was colder than normal too. As he wiped his finger on his leg, he continued along the water top.

His first crystal was for the base of the mountains. The crystal knew where it was headed and seemed to guide him. The navy crystal belonged here. It was to be placed at the foot of the mountains, under the river.

When Cyrus arrived to that spot, he knew it was time to dive in. The crystal was firmly in his hand. An ancient magic directed him into the depth of the river, and guided the navy gem firmly into the rocky bottom. Before he resurfaced, Cyrus saw the crystal connect to bedrock. Navy sparkles seeped onto neighboring rocks.

As quickly as it happened, it was over. For some strange reason the white marble columns flashed before his eyes. He shook his head and stared into the river.

Why would he see a column here now? He heard whispers from the river but could not fully understand them. Cyrus forced himself to focus on his current task. He had three more crystals to deliver.

He regarded the river and could see a rich, dark twinkle where he had just been. His heart beamed with pride and excitement. He knew what to do and he was being guided. Confidence was his new friend and he paddled furiously to the forest for his next gem.

Each crystal had the same effect. It guided Cyrus to the place it wanted, then merged in the river's bottom and spread just a little to leave a glimmer of hope.

Teal in the forest of Cazmal.

Next, the plains. Zulta's Plains claimed the turquoise gem.

Night drew closer as Cyrus circled the great land with his singular task.

After the Caves of Decalt were satisfied with the royal blue crystal, Cryus started his return to the falls.

24 Change

Mara felt the strength of the river as she floated and glided above the water. Marhilias touched her with warmth, and soft currents of water flowed along her body as she began her final change to being human.

Silent anticipation filled the air and Mara swallowed as she saw a reflection she had never seen before: her human reflection.

Her eyes were still silver and her hair still had a watery quality about it. Her face! Water was replaced by flesh and lips. A curious feeling swept through the river. Mara touched her cheek and wondered at the feel of her new skin. Was she human already?

She could hear the prophecies being whispered across the waves, "This is your task. Marcouera chose you to ensure Terramara thrives."

Mara thought, "Thank you Marcouera, thank you for choosing me."

Mara gazed upon her human self once more. Mesmerized by her own reflection, she found she could not draw her eyes away. The river began to stir. Light darted and flickered and marhilias buzzed with excitement.

Mara slowly leaned in, further and further, until she felt she had no control- the pool, the heart and home of the river was welcoming her. Mara felt dizzy. Blue crystals flashed before her eyes and slowly, she lost all sense of up and down.

Mara floated and twisted into an unknown world for some time.

Suddenly, SPLASH! Mara's human weight hit the water. She thrashed about, awkwardly realizing that for the first time, she had to *swim*. She slapped the surface and marveled at the ripple she created with her hand. She looked at her hand. *Her human hand.* She could *feel* the water!

Mara had always been at one with the water, but now she was separated. Swimming came easily to her, but it was all so new.

Another sensation came over her as she pulled herself to shore.

Mara shivered and realized what her first human sensation was.

Mara was cold.

25 The Gifts

Mara stepped out of the river onto the sandy banks and once she was dry, she stepped into her teal maybree. She had seen the humans in them, she knew how they worked. Her awkwardness subsided quickly and she stood confidently at the river's edge, smiling.

Next, she opened the robe. She touched it softly with her fingertips. It was incredible. Warm on the inside, delicate and silky on the outside. The color was a light blue and the bottom of the robe was embroidered waves with silver thread. There was three little buttons on each cuff and it flowed heavily to the ground. Mara admired the simple, yet amazing garment. It was a strange sensation to feel clothing.

Cyrus paddled in noisily. He could see her on the river's edge, tall and powerful in her teal robe. Her silver hair was stunning in the moonlight.

He called, "Mara!" and jumped from the board into the river. He landed waist high and surged towards her.

"Cyrus!" she beamed, "I'm here! Look at me! It's happened. I'm here."

She ran toward him and they met in the shallows. With mutual smiles, they embraced, laughing and speaking at once.

"You're human! It's amazing."

"It was amazing. I can't believe it's done."

Surprisingly, Mara did not feel awkward. Cyrus smiled and regarded the scene around her. The river was moving and flowing, except for the pool by Mara's feet near the shoreline. Here, the river was completely calm, like glass. It seemed to glow. Upon closer inspection,

Cyrus could see hundreds of marhilias quietly gazing at Mara, silently inspecting her human form. Mara followed his gaze down and smiled.

In the next moment, the river's water shot up into the air! Elevated, the water was lifted entirely out of its embankment. Stunned, the new couple turned to face the commotion. They took a step back and watched.

The currents mixed and mingled in the twilight. Water whipped back and forth in a mad fury. As quickly as it had begun, it was over. With a thunderous boom, the water slammed back down into its bank. The earth shifted. Mara and Cyrus felt small tremors in their feet. They stood silently and watched.

"Look," Mara whispered, "the current."

"It's coming from Mardivina now," Cyrus nodded. "It's happened. It's all happened, just as Marcouera said it would."

Their eyes sparkled in the glow of the river as dawn approached. Mara gazed adoringly at Cyrus and she saw the same feelings shining back. She noted the uniqueness of his eyes and wondered about her own. How marvelous his eyes looked!   Cyrus's voice broke her train of thought. "It's time to take you to the palace. There's a lot of people who want to meet you."

He offered his hand to Mara. Gracefully, she placed her hand in his. Despite her human form, there was a flowing quality about her that still reminded him of water. Perhaps it was her silver hair or the delicate way she moved. He gazed up at her face and realized her eyes were like the river- silvery and shimmering.

26 New Terrain

"We have to go to the Mardivina Mountains first," Mara stated.

Cyrus understood and nodded. The sun was just coming up, a new day had begun. They trekked to the mountains, walking and talking as they went.

"What was it like in the river?" Cyrus questioned.

"Peaceful. Busy. Fun." Mara shot back a round of answers then smiled. "It was so many things all at once. Every day blended into the next. It's a constant rush of water and movement. Right now, I feel exceptionally slow walking."

Cyrus furrowed his eyebrows at her statement and regarded their feet. "So, did you swim? Or fly? What was it like moving as a marhilia?"

She thought for a moment. "It was just easier. We flowed with everything in our path. I could bounce off a flower, run off a branch, slide into the river. Like water, I guess. I never had to, you know, step over a rock before. We never really rested, we didn't need to. We just flowed everywhere, all the time. It's so different moving as a human."

Mara gestured to the path in front of them and dramatically stepped over a rock. It wasn't a big rock, but she wanted to make her point. It was hard to explain what was different now. She thought about her movements, walking. She looked at the world around her and felt so small. Strange, she was so much bigger now! But the limitless travel and connections she once had were gone. They'd disappeared and Mara felt strangely alone.

Of course, she was also here with Cyrus. She felt

so strongly for him. But it wasn't the same. It was as though part of her was fulfilled and happy, and another part, sad and alone. The feelings mixed together insider her, leaving her unsure of what to do. These human emotions were so big and new, filling her mind in a way she couldn't imagine. She was brought back to their conversation as Cyrus began to talk.

"I bet it is strange," Cyrus said. "I can't imagine the changes! How different it all is for you. For me, now that you're human, it feels like you have always been human. Like there was no other 'Mara' before this."

He wondered what it would be like to be a marhilia. For a moment, he thought about what it would have been like if *he* transformed to *her* world. How awesome it would be to float and fly around. To be part of the river and to never be tired! That would be amazing.

But to feel the same as everyone? That would be difficult. He couldn't really understand that. He liked his independence. It was annoying when his father or his friends tried to push, or boss him around, or have their own way in an argument. Did marhilias argue?

Mara continued, "One of the weirdest things for me, actually, is the quietness I feel. I only have my own thoughts now. I am so curious about everything. I mean, nothing is new in this world to me, I know all the corners of the land. I know the flowers, the fields, the mountains. But back then, I was part of everything I touched. And now, I feel like an outsider. Here I am, walking *through* them but not *with* them. Does that make sense?"

Cyrus understood what she meant. Not entirely, of course, but the fact that he was royalty would always make him an outsider to the rest of Terramara.

He replied simply, "Yes, it makes sense. It makes a

lot of sense."

He smiled at her then took a small stride to let her take the lead. The path narrowed here and it was better navigated in single file. They walked along, quietly and comfortably.

When they arrived at the base of Mardavina, a vast mass of dryness met their eyes. Arid sand had settled tightly together. The desert was created, as foretold.

Stark and dry, the desert stretched for miles along the west side of the mountain's base. It signified the loss of Marcouera. When the magic transformed Mara, every last drop was drawn from this area.

The desert was formidable. Untended, it would take over all of Terramara, leaving it dry and lifeless.

They stood at the edge of the desert, side by side, silently taking in the vastness. It met the horizon in the distance, larger than either of them imagined. A tightness filled Mara's chest. Her duty would weigh heavily on her shoulders her entire human life. It would not be enough for her to care for the lands surrounding the desert. She would be responsible for teaching others to carry on after her. The future of Terramara depended on it.

But, she would not do it alone. Silently, she smiled at Cyrus. She would have him by her side, the beloved prince of the people. Together, they could water this world.

Cyrus could not believe the sprawling acrid space before him. It appeared overnight and he had never seen such unwelcoming lands. It was hard and dead. There were no trees, flowers, or life. He sighed at the size of the desert and turned to Mara.

"This is massive," he breathed.

Mara nodded. "Yes, I don't know what I imagined.

It is bigger than I thought. It seems so huge. But it's dryness can be managed. I know it can! It is my job to ensure the rest of Terramara thrives."

"You mean *our* job," Cyrus corrected.

Mara beamed. "Yes, our job. We can do it. I know the plans for this desert will come to us soon. Somehow."

"I know what you mean!" Cyrus exclaimed. "When I placed the blue crystals in the river, I had visions of the marble columns. It didn't make sense at the time, but I remember feeling they would be important...soon."

"Yes!" Mara exclaimed. "The columns have been in my thoughts too. I remember the words: *column, desert, teach, and water.* But to be honest, it's all still a little unclear."

"Same," Cyrus confirmed.

"We will figure it out. We will figure it out together," Mara declared.

They stood at the base of the mountain with quiet confidence. They knew they would be guided once more.

27 Warm Welcome

The people of Terramara met at the river each morning. They had all felt something shake in the night. They were curious and chattered excitedly about what they felt. Was it an earthquake?

They noticed that the river was different now, too. Where was the Slow Side? Overnight the river had changed. It now flowed *from* the mountain. Only one way!

It was almost noon by the time Cyrus and Mara returned to the palace. Curious onlookers smiled and nodded their heads as they saw the pair arriving hand in hand.

"Cyrus!" Johatt's voice broke Cyrus's trance.

Johatt strode toward them with a huge grin on his face and Lila at his heels. It was true! It was incredible. It had happened. The king had shared the recent events with his citizens.

Cyrus was returning to the palace now with a new companion by his side. Johatt could hardly believe it!

Lila and Johatt hurried toward Cyrus and Mara. His confident step slowed as Johatt took in the woman before him. Tall, slender, and graceful, Mara's human form was strong yet fluid. And her silver hair was like nothing he had ever seen before; it flowed with a water-like quality. He wanted to reach out and touch her hair to see what it felt like, but resisted. Her eyes sparkled with the same silver and twinkled with a friendly smile.

"Good morning," Johatt said.

Lila corrected, "Good afternoon!"

Cyrus welcomed them with warm embraces.

"Johatt, Lila, this is Mara."

"Mara," Johatt embraced her. To her surprise, it was quite pleasant. Mara hugged him in return and felt the warmth of his arms. Lila stepped forward and hugged her next. How wonderful! She felt Lila's hair tickle her cheek and she smiled. What was this warm feeling in her heart? This was all new! And different. Mara realized she still had so much to get used to.

"How wonderful to meet you. I can't believe you are here!" Johatt exclaimed.

Lila spoke, "We have heard so much about you! Oh, my, your eyes! They are stunning. I see the river flowing in them now! Sorry, I was going to be more... uh... uh..."

As Lila stammered, Johatt burst into laughter, "She's usually giving me elbows about etiquette! Then off she goes, blabbering on about your eyes the first time you meet!"

Lila blushed, giving Johatt a sharp elbow to his ribs.

"Ooof," he mumbled, with a small grin.

"It's okay," said Mara, smiling at the couple. "It is all so new. For us all! Cyrus and I spent the morning talking about what it's like to be marhilia, and what it's like to be human. Our worlds felt so close before. Every day we were together in the river, at the falls, Sandy Bend! But now that this transformation has actually happened, there's so much more to learn. It's a lot to take in. For us all. But I'm so pleased to meet you both."

Mara smiled at the outgoing couple. They stood quietly together for a while, until she sensed there was more to explain.

"I'm quite happy to share everything I know. I want my story to be known and understood."

"Thank you," Lila told her. She took in the beautiful woman before her and smiled her approval. "I can't wait to hear more. You must know it's been so hard to believe this, any of this …" Lila's smile faltered as she trailed off.

She was pleased for her friend's happiness, but wasn't completely trusting of Mara and the transformation. Not because she seemed untrustworthy, but because she was, well, a water sprite. Humans and water sprites had never really communicated with each other, let alone formed deep connections with one another. She closed her mouth and hoped that her fears were wrong.

Cyrus had been so passionate in his retelling of the woman in the river and though Lila wanted to show Cyrus support, a part of her struggled to believe the possibilities.   Things were different now. For here stood a woman, a real person, not just some fantasy from the river. It felt as though she had always been human. Lila was having trouble imagining that Mara had once been a water sprite. Her mind was just fine with meeting a new human, but to think she had once been part of the river! It was almost too much to take in.

She felt protective of her friend. Was Cyrus going to be okay? Was it all going to work out?

"Where is my father? I can't wait to introduce them." Cyrus had told Mara of his father's support and enthusiasm. "And Mara, we must prepare for a proper welcome for you. A festival for you to meet everyone!" Cyrus beamed.

"And wedding, if I may presume."Johatt winked at Mara.

Mara laughed aloud, her first human laugh. It was a beautiful sound, melodic and sweet. It brought even more smiles to those around her.

A wedding, she thought to herself. A human tradition to signify a union. It was new and unnecessary for Mara. She already knew that they were united. She felt the spirit-connection with Cyrus and knew their hearts were as one. She did not need anything more to make it true. It was simple. It was already done. But she smiled at the idea. She would have to learn their human ways and make them her own.

"Yes, a wedding," Mara agreed. "This will be my first time at a wedding."

Her statement sounded odd, for *who* had *never* been to a wedding before? The fact that Mara was so different had yet to sink in. It would take time. They would learn her differences, learn her history, and her past.

The humans would struggle to fully understand but they would try. And in time, they would embrace her. And she, would slowly become more and more human with every passing day.

The new couple led the way to the white palace, Johatt and Lila close at heel, leaving many curious onlookers in their wake. Had she really come from the river? The prince certainly seemed interested in her, as were many others. Never before had such a unique looking woman been seen.

Johatt jokingly made a comment about Mara's beauty on the way to the palace.

"Cyrus, shame on you! You told us how amazing your experience was in the river with Mara, we could scarcely imagine it, but you never told us what a beauty Mara is!"

Mara tilted her head towards this confident man with a smile. He made her feel welcomed in an easy, comfortable manner.

Lila smiled. "It's true, Mara, you are very beautiful. Johatt speaks his mind and can be a bit blunt sometimes."

At that, Lila jabbed him in the ribs again. Feigning injury, Johatt shrugged his shoulders and that sheepish grin returned.

"Mara, walk with me awhile and let's get to know one another," Lila began. "Tell me all about yourself."

28 New Friends

Mara smiled at this bold woman. She liked Lila. There was a friendly, easy quality about her, and she was not afraid to speak her mind. Mara appreciated that. It was strange to have to *wait* to hear what Lila thought and felt, though. Mara kept expecting a wave of oneness to fill them. She waited for a connection like she had in the river with the marhilias, but it never came.

Lila interrupted Mara's thoughts. She linked her arm into Mara's and looked expectantly at her. "Tell me of your life. What was it like before this?"

Mara smiled a knowing smile, this would not be the first time she would be asked this question. So simple, and yet, so complicated.

"My life as a marhilia is all I have known. There are no words for how long I was a part of the river. Human years are much different. I wonder if I will ever be able to explain it. There are no words to express the feeling of being *one* with water. In fact, I feel strange without water surrounding me. And yet, I also feel content now. I feel my new spirit, my human spirit, alive in me. I feel so many things I have never felt before."

"Like what?" asked Lila.

"I have never felt another *person.* I feel your arm now and it's strange. When we hugged earlier I could feel your arms and your warmth. Everything before always felt like water. There was so much water in me, around me, all the time. Even when I left the river, I still felt the same. Here, I feel different with every step."

Lila smiled. "You are very forthcoming. You don't hide anything. I like that."

Mara returned the smile. "Why would I? I come from the river's magic and it's all I've ever know."

"But magic in our world is not very common. This is a big deal. *You* are a big deal!" Lila explained.

Mara slowed her step and replied pensively. "I had not thought about that. But you knew marhilias were here, you humans always tried to see us or catch us! That magic has always existed between us."

Lila reasoned, "Yes, but it was only a small sliver of life for us – only at the river. And from one day to the next, who could say if we saw a sprite - or just a spray of water. The only magic that was really apparent were the two currents. Most rivers don't flow both ways in their lands. Marcouera was exceptional in that. But even then, when you grow up with it, it becomes less incredible. It becomes normal and it doesn't seem magic after a while."

Mara considered her statement and shook her head in disbelief. "For me, magic was alive in everything I did. The enchantments of the river were part of me, they flowed through me. The feeling of the whole river, the spirits within me. Those are the parts I miss the most now. The thing that makes me feel normal is feeling Cyrus's spirit calling me. I felt him calling me since the moment we first met."

"In the river?" Lila questioned.

"Yes." Mara smiled. So Cyrus had told Lila about their first experience together. It pleased Mara to know that Lila had Cyrus's trust. "Yes, in the river. My heart feels stronger when he is near. I know he feels it too. That is how we are connected. That is the magic that is still here."

Lila smiled. "Mara, that is not magic. That is love."

"Love?" Mara considered. "Love. Hmm. I have heard this word before. Many times in the human world. But I could not put it to any use as a marhilia. So, you are telling me that all humans *are* connected? Like marhilias?"

"No," Lila explained, "human love is different. Love can be many things. A mother can love a child and the child can love her mother. There is a connection with that love. A friend can love a friend, and there is a different connection with that. But I think the connection you feel with Cyrus is also love."

Mara thought about the explanation and nodded. "Yes, I have seen what you mean. Mothers, friends, and Cyrus. Yes, I would say we love each other. We love each other very much. But there is more to it. Cyrus calls to me...without words."

Mara stopped there, for she knew it was more. There was a connection beyond the human feeling. There was something deep within them, something that set them apart from all others. Instinctively, she knew they were the only two who felt this.

After a pause, Lila moved on, "We were really worried when Cyrus disappeared underwater for so long. It was an out of the ordinary incident for all of us. Cyrus is an excellent swimmer, but no human should be able to survive what he did. It's incredible. This whole thing is incredible. You, being a marhilia, now human. It's a lot for one to grasp in such a short time. And yet, when I speak and walk with you now, I cannot imagine you as a tiny water sprite." Lila shook her head in amazement at the woman before her and continued.

"You have a unique look about you, it does remind one of a marhilia. Your hair. And your eyes. Both are silvery and almost water-like. I'm tempted to touch your hair, just to convince myself it is not actually cascading water."

"It is a lot to explain. From meeting Cyrus in the river to my transformation and arrival in Terramara, it has all been quite fascinating for me too," Mara started.

"You speak with honesty. That is really the best way. It is hard for people to understand each other, even human to human sometimes. Everyone feels their own feelings and has their own thoughts. When we connect, it's extra special because it doesn't happen with just any-one. I can see how happy Cyrus is to have you here. He *calls* you, you say? What does that mean?" Lila asked.

"Does Johatt not call to you?" Mara inquired, "When I think of Cryus, I can feel his presence. I know if he is all right. I can feel him in my mind."

"Johatt and I do not connect like that. But our bond is strong. We find strength and comfort in one another. That is our bond, our love. Perhaps that is similar to this call you speak of," Lila suggested.

"Perhaps," Mara considered. "When I met Cyrus that day in the river, a connection was made immediate-ly. A connection that does not normally occur between human and marhilia. A bond between us was created and it has called me ever since. It may not be the exact same as Marcouera's call, and it may not be what you are de-scribing as 'love', but it the best way that I can explain."

"Yes," Lila mused. "I like your explanation. Love is one of the most wonderful of human emotions. It can fill your heart with immeasurable joy and happiness. And it has an incredible strength for when times are hard."

"Thank you, Lila," Mara declared. "I feel a bond with you now too. So, Lila, you and I also feel love."

Lila smiled proudly at Mara's assessment of her. "I am glad. Yes, we can love our friends. I liked you right away, too. That's the start of our bond. Once we get to know each other better our bond will become stronger." Lila realized that Mara was just starting to figure it all out.

Mara knew about connections and was learning her new feelings as a human. Mara smiled. She liked Lila's honestly and how she was unafraid to speak her mind. Mara appreciated her desire to understand and to share. There would never be another friend like Aida, but Lila's friendship made her happy. It was different than her connection with Cyrus, though.

Lila shifted their conversation. "So, what was it like? Being a marhilia?"

"It was truly wonderful. I loved the river and I always will. It will be different now, of course. I will never be a true part of the river again," Mara said, a slight pang tightening in her throat as she whispered the words aloud.

"Of course," Lila commiserated. "But tell me more of what it is feels like! What is it like to be part of the river? "

"The morning ride down the river was wonderful. Millions of marhilias, laughing and riding the river together," Mara recalled affectionately.

"Marhilias laugh? That's interesting. I never knew. I guess I never really thought about it," Lila commented.

"Oh yes! Aida and I …"

"Aida?" Lila interrupted. "I did not realize marhilias all had names. I knew you were to be called *Mara* for Cyrus had told me. I suppose I thought the name had been determined for you after the change into human.

You'll have to forgive my ignorance, but I had always imagined marhilias as simple creatures, like any other animal in the river or Terramara. I've never heard a marhilia speak or laugh and I never imagined them as individuals."

Lila's declarations were shocking to Mara as well. She had always just assumed that humans knew of the intricate lives of marhilias. She, after all, knew of their human ways. But then, she had access to all the lands and could go whereever she pleased, listen when she liked and see clearly all they did. Of course, humans were so big to her back then, nothing they did could be missed!

Mara stopped and glanced back at the river. She heard human voices greeting one another, sharing stories, and laughing.

She heard many voices, but not what she expected. Mara focused harder on the river and was stunned by what she could no longer hear. Where there once had been thousands of marhilias laughing, giggling and playing, now, all she heard was the soft thundering of water and humans.

29 The Palace

Arriving at the palace, Mara couldn't believe how different the world appeared through human eyes. It had always seemed huge and grand, but now she was able to take in details in a new light.

Long slender columns lined the road leading to the palace, but each column had been intricately carved out of white marble to look like flowing waves. There were at least fifty on each side; Mara lost count as she went. She looked down at her robe and re-examined the embroidered waves. She noted the similarity between the stitching and the columns.

Lila watched Mara's hand trace her embroidered waves. "We love the water. It's a big part of our lives. We love marhilias. I know I said our life wasn't as magical as you had hoped. But we still adore the water sprites."

Lila gestured up. Mara's eyes followed her arm. Atop each column were carved images of marhilias. Mara marveled at how well these carvings showed their true likeness. They were difficult to see at first, as they were entirely white like the rest of the columns, but Mara was sure that small joyous faces were present in the intricately carved marble.

Beyond the crystal columns were beautiful gardens. Mara smiled at her old memories of the garden. Gentle flowers of every color, waiting for their morning greeting from eager marhilias, swayed in the breeze. How different the flowers looked from the perspective she had now! A small girl ran to greet Lila and Mara. She handed a fistful of flowers to Mara in a shy childlike welcome.

"Thank you," Mara told her. The girl blushed and

ran away.

Lila nodded her approval towards the young girl and Mara inspected the daisies in her hand. How small they seemed now. She could once hide inside one petal and now she could easily hold an entire bouquet in her hands. The firm stem rolled between her fingers and she inspected the velvet petals.

Mara looked up to see a colorful mosaic of blues. Turquoise rocks and stones glistened in the sun. Marble columns framed the entrance and three smooth steps created a perfect semi-circle around the palace.

The palace itself was light blue marble towering in layers. Each circle on top of the next one was reduced in size by a foot or so, leaving the highest layer a thin blue spear towering towards the sky.

Oval windows were carved in the four base levels of the palace. The windows had no glass, but water cascading in perfect sheets. The sound of soft water enveloped the palace and a serene feeling overcame Mara as she walked up the stairs.

Breathless at the sight of the glimmering castle, Mara's attention was stolen by the beauty around her. Cyrus's hand found hers again, firmly grasped it and led her up the stairs. Mara followed willingly, but was glad of his hand offering guidance.

"Come on, I'm excited for you to officially meet my father now."

30 The King

King Anzoil waited anxiously, excitement buzzing in his mind. Cyrus had left in such a hurry after the crystals were removed. He had grabbed a fine tunic and teal maybree. The king had stepped forward with the offering of a beautiful, special robe. It was Queen Zulta's.

"Are you sure?" Cyrus had asked, his heart skipping with joy.

His father had nodded firmly and gladly gave it to his son. With a quick hug, Cyrus left and it had been over a day since they'd seen one another.

Mara met the King of Terramara, wearing the special robe. The meeting was mutually affectionate. Mara liked the king's straightforward and kind manner and she felt at ease around him at once. For his part, the king was more than pleased to meet such a charming young lady who had at long last encapsulated his son's heart. The fact that their union was filled with ancient magic and historical change made the king beam even brighter. His approval at the pairing was apparent and Mara was happy.

"Mara, it delights me to see Cyrus so thrilled with your arrival. I couldn't be more pleased about it." King Anzoil beamed. "And might I add, that robe becomes you."

"Your highness, it is an honor to meet you. I am glad that you are pleased with my arrival." Mara bowed to the king.

"My dear, there is no need for formality here. You are to call me Anzoil," The king dismissed his title light-heartedly.

"Thank you," Mara said, smiling at the great man.

She regarded her robe again with tenderness. It was exceptionally beautiful.

"It belonged to Cyrus' mother. She was an incredible person." Anzoil smiled Mara.

He regarded his son, standing proudly and smiling broadly at Mara. Cyrus was proud to present her to his father. Anzoil liked Mara. He wanted to know more about this intriguing young woman.

"And so, Mara, we know you hail from the river. It wouldn't take a fool to see that you are not from here. I have never seen someone with hair so silver and eyes to match," the king told her.

"I have a unique background," she confirmed with a laugh. "That is true. I am the only one of my kind. I come from Marcouera. It sounds strange to say that out loud, that I come from Marcouera. For me, it's a whole different world, not simply the river." Mara paused to gauge the reaction in the king's blue eyes.

She knew the king was aware of her history, and she was not about to keep her life's story secret for anyone. She was proud of Marcouera, loved the marhilias and would not soon forget what she had so recently left behind. The king silently regarded her statement and nodded thoughtfully.

"It is hard to believe, even though I have been prepared for it. And yet, how could anyone doubt you?" Anzoil was delighted with the refreshing honesty Mara presented. "And just look at you. It truly is astonishing. Your eyes in particular. Your eyes are breathtaking, they do remind me of the river."

Mara smiled at his response. It was a relief to see how well she was being welcomed by her new world.

And she, too, wondered about her eyes – were they really so special?

Mara and Cyrus told the king the story of her transformation.

"The combined strength of all the marhilias joined together for one last time for Cyrus and I to meet and for me to be transformed. And now, Marcouera is no more. The strength of her spirit is gone and there are only a few marhilias left. They will help for as long as they can, but eventually..." she trailed off, her face darkening with the realization of that enormous loss.

Up to this point, she had only experienced the joy of her new connection with Cyrus and the wonderful people she had met. With growing sadness, she realized her connection with the river was gone. She could not hear it calling. She could not feel Aida, either. Or any marhilias for that matter.

"Excuse me," she whispered, turning toward the river. Understanding, the king put a gentle hand on her shoulder.

"Maybe you want some time at the river?" he asked. "We can get better acquainted later. There's plenty of time for that."

Graciously, she smiled and nodded.

"Shall I come with you?" Cyrus asked gently.

Mara nodded again.

31 Farewell

"I am thinking about Aida. I never thought about what would happen to her. I mean, I know she was happy for me and I remember every moment of the underwater ceremony so I know she understands. She's a marhilia and they all understand. It's just…" Mara trailed off.

How could she explain it?

She was happy to be here, happy to be with Cyrus, happy to be human. But she had also just lost many sisters, her home, and a comfort that could never be duplicated. Or fully explained. Already her time as a human had shown her how different it would be. She now had so many thoughts in her mind, so many ideas and feelings, and there was no connection attached to them. It was strange, she wasn't sure if she would ever get used to it.

Cyrus waited for her to collect her thoughts.

"It's just," she sighed, "I will miss our time together in the river. I will miss her when she is gone forever."

"Will she know you?" Cyrus asked, "I mean, I thought marhilias were all the same. I am learning so much."

"Yes, Aida is still with the river. She played a big part in the transformation. Marcouera used Aida's spirit to speak to me. And it was Aida's essence that came to you in the library. Aida will be one of the last ones remaining because of that."

Worry flickered in her silvery eyes and she slowed her pace. As much as she wanted to return to the river and see it with her new human form, she also felt something missing: her friend. She wondered about Aida, would they find each other?

Aida had felt her own solo feelings while Mara was being transformed. She had been separated from the river, too. And she had felt alone in feeling the strange, new powers from the enchantress.

Mara only had a glimpse of Aida's feelings before she turned human. But she knew that it felt awesome. She also knew that it felt lonely for she had experienced something on her own too. Mara longed to see her old friend.

A day! It had only been one day.

Mara stared hard into the river but it was silent. Mara was gripped by uncertainty. She squatted by the river and dipped her hand in. Feeling water was odd.

Liquid dripped off her fingers and she concentrated on the glistening drops. Mara brought her wet hand up in front of her face and watched the tiny droplets dripping fall back into the river.

She squinted and leaned in closer to her hand. A quick spritz shot up and splashed her in the face. On her fingertip, a small droplet quivered. A slow smile crossed Mara's face as she saw her friend. No words were said for a moment and both creatures sat in wonder of the other.

Mara investigated the water droplet on her fingertip. She slowly twisted her wrist right, then left. It was a water drop with a tiny orange glow.

"You're here," Mara whispered with glee.

"Where else would I be?" Aida retorted with a cheeky smile.

Mara was relieved. They could understand each other! Mara was human and Aida was a sprite but they could still talk. Their friendship was not lost after all. She flashed Aida a huge grin.

"It's happened," Mara told her. "I'm human. Can you believe it?"

Aida nodded. "I see that. It's so strange to be able to talk to you! I mean, I'm so glad we can. I miss you already."

"I miss you, too," Mara echoed. "It's so weird not being connected to you!"

"I know." Aida nodded. "I keep expecting you to reappear in my thoughts. I'm so happy we can still talk to each other."

Aida twinkled in her excitement and took in her friend's new form. The two delighted in their reunion.

"So, how do you feel?" Aida changed the subject.

"I feel okay," Mara started then paused. "I can't hear the river anymore."

"Oh," said Aida, frowning and at the same time, understanding. She knew because she also could not feel Mara.

They sat in silence for a moment, just taking one another in. Mara could not stop marveling at the shimmer, colors and reflections of this tiny droplet on her finger. How it seemed to glow, how there was no shape, just a bead of water with energy. How different Aida looked to her now, simple, small, and perfect.

In turn, Aida studied the human, realizing that she had never sat on a human fingertip. It was usual to come and go, flit and fly, swoosh around, but this was different. She started at the top, admiring Mara's hair as it moved in the light breeze.

Aida took in Mara's face and marveled at how big her eyes were. And how expressive! She could see her friend admiring her- studying her as she sat on a fingertip.   "I do feel happy," Mara told her finally. "It's strange. I feel like I've always been human now. Everything about this body and shape feels so normal. And yet, I remember the river. I remember the call. I remember our days together. It's just not the same as it once was. I don't feel like *part* of the water. I just remember it now, like a memory."

Aida nodded, but couldn't fully understand. She knew she could no longer feel Mara's presence, she knew that the transformation had depleted much of the marhilia magic.

Aida was one of the last sprites in the waters of Terramara.

There were once thousands of marhilias and now only a handful remained. A light sadness washed over Aida as she considered her friend's disconnection. Things would be different for all of them, but it had to happen.

Suddenly, Aida sprang from Mara's finger and landed on her nose.

"Oh!" Mara started and looked down at her friend, a tiny bead sitting on her nose.

They shared a smile. And with a little slide, launch and jump, Aida flew through the air and landed back into the river with the tiniest of ripples following her.

Mara ran into the river laughing. "Come back! I'll get you!"

Cyrus, who had been waiting down further on the bank, saw Mara and her good spirits. He jumped in at once. A huge smile on his face, he arrived where Mara was splashing and flapping about.

"Everything okay?" Cyrus smiled for he knew that it was.

"YES!" Mara shrieked as she batted and patted the river. "I just owe someone some good splashes."

Cyrus joined in. Splashing and shooting water towards the river, joining Mara's playful attack. Before long, they realized they were only splashing one another. Fits of laughter, water everywhere, the couple eventually stopped. Out of breath, waist deep in the water, and smiling.

"And now?" Cyrus asked. "How are you now?"

Mara regarded the water in front of her, gazed along the winding river and beamed at him.

"I'm good. I saw her. Aida's here and she's okay." Mara breathed out relief, "We can head back to the castle now."

As the new couple returned from the river, citizens of Terramara tentatively approached. Cyrus welcomed them in, and introduced Mara as they flowed back to the palace. Mara's charm and ease won the hearts of all she met, and by the time the palace was in sight, a fairly large procession arrived with the two. Patiently answering the people's questions and appreciating their eagerness to learn about her, Mara shared freely all she knew and had known. As a marhilia and now, as human.

When they arrived at the palace, Mara smiled at Cyrus.

"I have an idea."

32 The Invitation

An invitation went out from King Anzoil to all the citizens of Terramara. This invitation was like no other, for a story accompanied it.

Mara's idea was to send out their wedding invitations along with their enchanted tale. The story of her life and the river, Cyrus, the transformation and magic.

"I want people to know and understand who I am," she told Cyrus on their way back from the river. "It's important to me. Meeting your father helped me see how unique our situation truly is. And just now, seeing Aida again, I want to make sure the marhilias are never forgotten. The people who walked home with us had so many questions, so many things I didn't realize were unknown or new. I want the world to know what it's like in the river. The marhilias are almost gone and I want everyone to know who we truly were."

Both Cyrus and the king thought it was a wonderful idea. Word had already spread about Prince Cyrus and Mara meeting. Slivers of truth were being mixed with legends and fairy tales. The stories grew as the news covered the land. The wedding invitation would set the record straight.

The king gathered his poets and writers, and their tale was put into script. Scrolls were sent out to everyone. His minstrels put it to song and set about to sing and share in the villages. The finest artists in the land were called upon and Anzoil dedicated both walls in the palace's south garden to be celebrated with a mural of their story.

The legend of Cyrus and Mara had begun. People

grew excited to meet this wondrous new human. A girl who had lived thousands of years under water, *was* water and now a human. And not just any human, one who would wed their prince. Imagine!

The decrees went out within the week and news of their story brought joy and excitement to all the citizens. The buzz throughout the kingdom was unstoppable. What did she look like? What would she sound like? Was she capable of ruling? They had learned of her kindness and history, but so many questions were still unanswered.

They looked forward to the wedding, festivities and grand party, but most of all, meeting the woman from the river.

33 The Bad News

Amidst the celebration and joy of Mara's first week, a man rushed in, harried, and in shock. Clearly exhausted, he went directly to the king and spoke in hushed, hurried tones. Something was amiss. The commotion caused by the man began to draw more and more attention, and soon everyone involved in the festivities paused to find out what was going on.

Cyrus marched over to his father and joined the conversation. From a distance, Mara could see a small argument ensuing. Shortly after, Cyrus searched the room and when his eyes met Mara's, he beckoned her over.

Mara ushered herself through the crowd to get to the three men.

"Anzoil, I am telling you, there is a desert on the west side of Mardavina," the man said, "and I don't mean any small thing. Terramara is at risk."

A whispered hush went through the crowd. A desert? Surely not. The marhilias wouldn't let that happen. Where did it come from? Was the river okay? Was it Mara's fault? Terramara had never had any issues with water and greenery before her change.

As quickly as they embraced Mara, people began to look suspiciously at her and slowly they backed away. Their distance allowed Mara to get to Cyrus and the king.

"Father, you know…" Cyrus was interjecting.

The man exploded. "The desert is the beginning of the end!"

"Please," Mara began. "I can explain it."

"You will not…" the man burst, then he looked at Mara and stopped mid-sentence. Her striking silver hair and eyes were unlike anything he had ever seen.

He spluttered, "Who are...? What...?"

King Anzoil spoke. "Grayson, let me introduce you to Mara, Daughter of Marcouera. Mara, this is Grayson, one of my most trusted advisers and friends."

Mara nodded her greeting. Unable to move, Grayson stood staring, speechless.

"Please, let me explain about the desert," she tried. "I can explain everything that has happened in the last few days. Furthermore, I know what will happen next."

She spoke directly to Grayson. The citizens of Terramara had ceased their merry-making and were wholly focused on the events unfolding with the king and Mara.

"My friends," King Anzoil addressed the crowd. "We have all met and been quite taken with the lovely Mara. There is more to her story and we will explain it all. As most of you have heard, my most trusted friend, Grayson, has come with news of a large desert in Terramara. But please, believe me, it will all be okay. Mara and Cyrus can explain it all."

Puzzled, Grayson muttered to the king, "You knew about this..."

The king nodded, stepped aside and gestured for Mara to speak.

34 An Explanation

Relieved to be supported by the king, Mara stood tall.

"I will tell you all the story of the desert," she began. "It starts with the enchantment of the river. Years ago, when the hundred days and nights of fire plagued this land, Marcouera gave all her strength to settle the storms and create the river. She sacrificed her body but her spirit lived on. It fell into millions of pieces, droplets of water within the river. Those pieces were us, the marhilias."

Citizens began to protest, "Yes, we know this!"

"We read the story..."

"The wedding invitation..."

"But how does this explain the desert?"

"How big is the desert?"

"Please, let me continue," Mara begged.

Cyrus stepped forward and stood firmly beside her.

"Yes, the invitation," Mara continued. "It explained my history but it did not speak of the foretold desert."

Cyrus interrupted. "When we sent out the invitation, we wanted you to know the story of Mara and Cyrus. Our story. I wanted you to know who she was, and why she had suddenly appeared and why I love her so. We decided that the wedding invitation was not the time to tell you about the desert."

Subtle gasps went through the crowd as they realized... the prince knew!

"Yes, that's correct. Both father and I knew of the desert. I, myself, have laid eyes on it," Cyrus continued. "It is formidable. But there is hope. That hope lies in Mara, myself and the remaining marhilias. And you.

Each citizen."

"So you have seen it?" Grayson demanded. "You know of its great expanse. Cyrus, it covers so much of Terramara. How? Why? I don't understand!"

Mara took over. "Marcouera's spirit was dying. If my transformation did not occur, all of Terramara would have died with her. Over time, all the water in this great land would have dried up. The waterfall would have dwindled and eventually stopped. The Sandy Banks would have crept across the plains, and the mountains of Mardivina would have crumbled into the fields. Dust and sand everywhere. And no water. It has been years since the fires, but her remaining strength could not sustain Terramara any longer. The ancient magic that brought me here is the last of its kind."

Silence was heavy among the citizenry, as it hung on her every word. Not a murmur could be heard.

"The reason I have been connected with Cyrus is to share my skills. I used to water the lands with a team of marhilias using dewdrops and mist. As a human, I will water the world differently. I know how to use water to care for this land. I have the experience of a marhilia, but I cannot do it alone."

"Mara has come to help us all," Cyrus told them. "Marcouera knew that we would need the river's water and a marhilia's mind to help sustain our world."

The King stepped forward to join the couple. "As well, the man you know as my son, Prince Cyrus, is more than you realize. His eyes contain the silvery-blue of the river; there is a water spirit within him - legends from ancient times speak of a man with these eyes. My son is precisely the human Marcouera was waiting for. As Cyrus grew and spent his days in the river, Marcouera grew to know him and the ancient voices of her sisters spoke to her, guiding her to this conclusion. It's hard for me to believe this legend is coming true before my very eyes. With my own son!"

"It's true," Mara told him, grateful for the kings support. "I, Mara, am a direct descendant of Marcouera herself and my eyes confirm that my lines are from the river's heart. Only a little while ago, Cyrus and I met there. Shortly after, my amazing transformation took place and now here I am. Marhilia, in human form now and forever. Your prince and I have been linked together. Our bond can neither change nor disappear."

"But what about the desert?" Grayson interrupted.

"Yes, the desert," Mara began. "The desert was going to happen whether I arrived or not. The final transformation took a lot of power and that is why a desert has emerged. Water had to be pulled from the land to complete my human transformation. It is my task to teach you to care for the desert, and more precisely, all of Terramara. Watering the land is up to us now."

"Well," Grayson huffed, his left eyebrow raised in doubt. "That sounds fine and good for you, but what assurance do we have that you will commit to this task? The desert is monstrous! It would have been better if you'd have stayed in the river."

A worried outcry spread through the crowd. Grayson was well known and well trusted; his concern was enough to set off worry.

"Please, let me finish," Mara told them, standing her ground. The king gestured with his hands for silence and Mara continued. She felt a wet warmth on her hand again and glanced down to see Aida sitting there, silently supporting her. It gave her strength.

"The marhilias that remain will slowly lose their ability to spread water throughout the land. Soon, they will lie deep in the river and no longer water the land. My task…"

"Our task," Cyrus interrupted with certainty.

Aida approved of his support.

"Our task." Mara smiled with relief at Cyrus, thankful for his strong, and true bond. "Our task is to take over the watering of the lands. Terramara needs water. The marhilias are dying. You ask what keeps me here? It's my bond with Cyrus and love for Terramara. We have a connection that cannot be explained, it can only be felt. We both feel it. I will never leave his side. That is a piece of the river's magic that will never die."

Cyrus clasped her hand. "And I will never leave Mara's side!" he boomed. "She is right. Our bond is deep. It flows through every ounce of my being. I feel Mara's heart in my own heart. We are here, together. Forever."

A murmur went through the crowd. A buzz of questions, whispers of worry, and concern emerged.

"How can we do this?"

"Terramara is too big!"

"Will the water run out?"

"How will we manage?"

"Where will the marhilias be?"

"Who knows if this is true?"

Once again, Anzoil comforted his citizens. "Citizens of Terramara, my friends, listen. All that has come to pass has come for a reason. This desert will not be the downfall of Terramara. Mara has spoken, and she has said that Terramara will thrive under her care. With Cyrus. I have no doubts of my son's capabilities. I have no doubts of Mara's truths. She, Cyrus, Grayson and I will visit the desert tomorrow," Anzoil told them. "I believe that will put many minds at ease."

The king pointedly looked at Grayson, who slowly released his breath and nodded in agreement to the king's suggestion.

Mara smiled. "Good idea. We have much to do tomorrow and in the days to come. The marhilias have not left us yet."

"Why didn't you tell us?" someone demanded.

Lila stepped forward. "Cyrus wanted to, but we told him to wait until after the wedding. We wanted to celebrate their marriage, and wait until everyone had met Mara and seen what she is really like."

Cyrus went on. "Perhaps we were wrong to wait. We cannot go back now, we can only go forward. We can take anyone who is interested along with us tomorrow to the desert."

Murmurs of agreement went through the crowd.

"Oh, yes, I'd go."

"I don't want to wait."

"I'll be there.'

"You are all welcome. We will show you what we know. We will learn together from Mara and the river. There are places throughout the land that need more water, and places where water is not so greatly required. Everyone must learn and everyone can assist. We will not lose our great water source, our river will be here."

A wave of ease settled over the people. Even Grayson seemed satisfied with the answers, and the plan for the next day.

"Tonight is meant for celebrating. We are still planning a great wedding in a short time! Let's return to our music and dancing," the king concluded. "Tomorrow, those willing will visit the desert with us and we will discuss the task at hand."

He patted Grayson on the back and invited him to walk along with a gesture of his hand. Grayson obliged, for as long as he had known this king and been friends with him, he had never been given reason to doubt him.

Slowly, conversations resumed among the guests, and though the topics continued to swirl around the union of water and land, the tone of the evening gradually became lighter and joyous once more.

35 The Visit

The next day, a group of fourteen men and women joined Mara to visit the desert. They brought lunches with them and set out on the four hour journey. It was a pleasant walk, and they chatted about the upcoming wedding. There was, of course, an anticipation about seeing the desert but nobody talked about it just yet. The time went quickly and before they knew it, they arrived at the base of the Mardivina mountains.

They stood at the edge of the desert and regarded its vastness. For a moment, there was no sound. It appeared to go on forever. Dry, brown sand covered the barren land before them. It was flat, treeless, and you could feel heat radiating from the ground. Small teams of marhilias flitted on the desert's edge, ensuring it would expand no further. But once the sand began, the flurry of watering activity stopped.

Cyrus spoke first. "So, you see. It is large."

They nodded amongst themselves with murmurs of agreement.

Their faith in Mara and Cyrus was bigger than their worry.

"Where do we begin?" asked Grayson, "It seems like a huge task. And one that we are not well versed in. The river has always cared for our land. The marhilias have ensured it was green. And now, it's our job. We do not carry water with us. So, how is this to be done?"

"Yes, you are right," Mara told him. "We are not like the water sprites. We don't have unlimited water at our fingertips. It's odd to me to think that was once normal. I could not imagine water trailing down my human hand now!"

They smiled with her attempt at humor, and tensions lifted.

Mara continued, "There are ways to make the river work with us. We must set about troughs to let the water flow. When the water is directed here, we can manage it on and around the desert."

"What ...vessel, what .. pipes… do we use?" asked Johatt.

"Yes, yes, how will we do it?" asked Lila. The others added more rapid fire inquiries.

"We could use water bags?"

"Or buckets?"

"No, those are too small."

"Will we do this every day?"

"It's going to be a lot of water."

They went searching for solutions, trying to determine how to transport the water.

Mara smiled at their enthusiasm. "We will use the columns. The white marble ones."

Everyone looked at her in amazement.

"The columns?" King Anzoil asked pensively. He rubbed his chin as he thought about it. Slowly, he began to nod as he recalled the hollow four.

Mara kept explaining. "Yes, the columns. They were originally created by the ancient magic of these lands. They were lovingly carved and have been a special structure all these years. They have a smoothness to them, incredible carvings of sprites and water but there is more to them than meets the eye."

Curious, the all focused on Mara and waited for her to proceed.

"The columns are hollow. They must be taken down

and split at their seams. They will create the perfect trough for water. We will line them in rows across the land."

A few gasps were heard.

"They're hollow?" Grayson asked.

"Yes," Mara answered with a grin.

"It's true," the king confirmed. "When the crystals came out of the four coloumns, you could see right down them. I put my hand in one to feel!"

"So, we build our troughs with the columns?" asked Grayson.

"Yes," Cyrus jumped in. "The plans for the columns, the desert and how to build it is all in my mind too. Both Mara and I saw the imagery when we were underwater. I did not realize I knew so much, but now, as you ask me questions about it, visions of what to do are flowing through my mind. More than visions. I see answers and solutions."

As soon as the group returned to the palace, they were eager to inspect the columns. There was lively chatter on the palace grounds as they shared what they had seen and what was to happen next. People touched the smooth, white columns in disbelief. How could they be hollow? And, even if they were, how could they manage to lower them? Never mind cutting them in half and moving them? So many questions!

Cyrus and Mara shared a knowing smile; they both knew what was coming. They knew the magic that was waiting. And they knew when it would occur.

On their wedding day.

36 Preparing

For the wedding, Mara and Cyrus had a special request. The people of Terramara began at once. They were to build stands from the trees to fortify their future irrigation system. The stands were to be crafted in an 'x' and made only from branches that contained blue or silver. Any other tree colors would be left to bear fruit in the forest.

And so, the people worked relentlessly in teams cutting, building, and binding. The x-shaped bases were strong and beautiful. Different shades of blues and silvers mixed in haphazard fashion. The creative colors did not impact their structure; the stands were solid and strong.

The few marhilias that remained flitted and floated by, watching the busy humans. Aida, in particular, spent a lot of time in Cazmal these days. She scampered up her favorite pink and yellow tree that would not be used for building. She sat in safety and watched the humans working as a team.

She felt a pang of jealousy as she watched Mara smiling, directing, working, and laughing. She missed her friend. She missed the feeling of having many friends.

And for Aida, the feeling was strong. Since her time as Marcouera's voice, she, too, could feel things in isolation. She could feel things that the other remaining sprites did not. She wished she could return to her old ways, with Mara, in the river. It was not nice, this feeling of alone. She frowned as she looked on, her tiny body sinking into a yellow branch. As she sank into the branch, her orange simmered with anger and the branch's color slowly darkened to a deep, tawny shade.

Below, the buzz of productivity was high. Johatt and Lila directed crews of workers to trees and branches. Searching for what would be used, sometimes just a branch or two, sometimes a large trunk. They needed hundreds of stands and the work had only begun.

Mara and Cyrus drafted a map of Terramara and marked where they would need to be set. Grayson and Anzoil joined them in directing the assembly and delivery. Stands were taken to the Plains of Zulta, the palace, and to Mara's Desert.

Each day, the humans continued their plans. Each day, they joyfully built and transported bases for their future. And each day, Aida sat in the large tree and scowled.

Mara sighed with satisfaction. The work was going splendidly. She walked a bit further into the forest and smiled at a memory.

"What's your favorite tree?" In front of her was Aida's – the largest one with pink and yellow.

Mara's smile turned into a puzzled look. She was sure this was the tree, the one that Aida had loved so much, but how could it be? The one Aida selected was vibrant yellows and pinks, it stood out and was magnificent. The tree in front of Mara now seemed to be the one, only it had turned into a soft, sad shade of brown.

She sighed at the change but thought no more of it. It was sad that the tree wasn't as bright as before, but it seemed insignificant. She returned to her human crew and began to work. It would be another week before enough stands were made for the project.

37 The Celebration

When the stands were finally complete Mara and Cyrus were excited. Now they could be married. Plans were made for the very next day! The palace hosted in grand style between the place and the Grand Falls. It was an exciting day for all. There were celebrations of all kinds: competitions, water games and events by the falls, food and festivities.

The feast was grand; tables of mouth-watering foods and delicacies, and multicolored fruits lay in heaping bowls. The smell of fresh fruit sweetly perfumed the air, and people enjoyed the occasion with contented ease, eating as they wished, dipping into the river to swim, and dancing to a delightful mix of merry music.

Life in Terramara was not formal. All were welcome to the palace at any time, and a royal wedding was no exception. The king meandered through the crowds easily, talking to everyone by name, asking about their work and families. It was a comfortable celebration with friends.

There was a special energy about this day. The king's smile radiated from his face with pride. Citizens were light-hearted and full of laughter. Everyone was in a joyous mood.

When the time for vows arrived, they gathered at the river bank across from the falls. Prince Cyrus made his grand entrance with Johatt by his side. Both were dressed in silver maybrees with just a touch of blue on their coordinating tunics. They made their way to the king, waiting to do the ceremony at the river. Both men smiled and laughed as they went, sharing nods with citizens who were there to celebrate. Cyrus arrived to his father's side and they embraced.

"My son," Anzoil beamed. "How handsome and happy you look. This day brings me so much joy."

Cyrus grinned back. Glancing up at the waterfalls, he drew in a breath.

There was Mara, lovely Mara, in mist and water, coming down the white marble rocks. A huge smile filled her face; she was magnificent.

A silver and white maybree fit her strong figure. Her tunic was full length and draped gently to the rocks at her feet. Blue jewels lined a satin sash around her waist, and matched the jeweled line of crystals in her hair, holding back the silvery locks from her face. She was a river princess, made of water, gliding along in blue and silver. She was, of course, human now, but her movements were so elegant, Mara appeared to float. She arrived in front of the king and bowed.

Cyrus realized this was the joy he had been searching for. He reached for Mara's hand and squeezed it. She closed her fingers warmly around his hand and looked up into his eyes, as her own twinkled with delight.

A soft, damp feeling came between their fingers and Mara looked down. She smiled as she recognized Aida. Mara brought her hand up to her face and grinned. Aida smiled back, and flung herself back into the river. Mara chuckled at her friend's silly ways, and looked around for her briefly.

Aida was nowhere to be seen so Mara turned her attention back to Cyrus. Music played and people watched as the couple was wedded together by their beloved king.

38 White Columns

Their anticipation of what would happen next made them both giddy with excitement. Mara and Cyrus were wed, and they knew it was only a matter of time before the next act would begin.

"Friends," Cyrus announced. "We need your attention!"

Music slowed, people shuffled closer and waited for their prince to continue.

"It's tradition to dance and celebrate at a wedding and we thank you for your shared joy with us. On this day, the prophecy of the white columns will come to pass. In the past few weeks, you have all met Mara, seen the magic before you and noticed differences in the river. Soon, we will prepare for the biggest adjustment of all. The marhilias are going to fade into the heart of the river, and we must water Terramara. The great white columns are the answer. As you know we have been busily preparing for this day. And today, they will be moved."

An excited chatter went through the crowd. Everyone looked at the colossal columns and wondered the same thing: How will this be possible? Anticipation filled the air as they speculated and shared ideas. What magic was coming!? They had already witnessed so much this week!

There was an excitement in the air as Mara continued. "We must go, in teams, to the desert, the forest and the plains. The heart of the river will guide the columns. We must be ready to embrace them, to set them into our great stands."

Crews had already been arranged and the people

went enthusiastically to their designated areas. What would it be like? How was it going to happen? There was excited chatter as they dispersed to the four corners of the land.

39 The Heart of the River

Cyrus and Mara climbed the Great Falls. They reached the top and prepared to dive in. They had been married by King Anzoil, and their union was recognized by all in the land.

But this incredible couple, on this day, had another ceremony to attend before the final great magic could occur. Their union must be received by the Heart of the River for the next phase to begin.

Mara squeezed Cyrus's hand firmly. He smiled at her and without a word, they plunged into the deep. The plummeted with the falls and hit the water's surface. Down, down, down, they dove. Their strong legs kicked as they forced their way deeper.

The river's bottom was in sight. They reached out their arms and shared a glance. Finally, the dark rocks were just below them. Their fingers touched them at the same time.

They paused underwater, looking at one another, waiting. They needed no air for they were in the river's magic, hovering just above its shimmering heart.

Within moments, sparkles from the four crystals shot down through the river, like streams of ribbon. And all the marhilias- what was left of them- circled and surfaced, leaving the couple behind.

Blue ribbons of water shot out of the river. People started at the thundering noise of the water and watched in awe as glowing streams whizzed around Terramara.

A swarm of silver and blue, marhilias and ribbons encircled the first few majestic columns. They snaked around it from top to bottom. The marhilias trickled right down the center of the length on both sides. With a white glow, each column split seamlessly and perfectly in two. The airy water, hovering above land, carried each piece of the column through Terramara.

The humans were amazed, watching this impossible feat. Watching their heavy pillars be handled as though they were delicate blades of grass. The magical ribbons from the water appeared soft and gentle, but they had the strength to cradle the solid marble. Hovering through the air, just above the humans, the columns flew to the four corners of the land!

As the first column was leveled and lowered towards the stands, the first crew snapped into action. They steadied and directed it with their hands, ensuring it landed between a series of strong stands.

The crystal ribbons and marhilias began working faster now. Column after column floated with magic water and sprites. One by one, they filled the stands that lined the plains and the desert. Aida was among them; she could feel the power from the crystals and it felt like there were millions of marhilias once more. Her heart soared and she lost herself in the magic current of blues, carving into marble and lifting gigantic white beams. At times it felt like she was directing them, like she was the one in control of the water's great surge of power.

Hours passed as columns were engineered free from their bases, slivered in half and carried to the lands. And all the while, the royal couple hovered in the heart of the river, silent, still and holding fast to the remains of the river's heart.

They could feel a tingle, a warmth surrounding them in the deep. The watery figure of Aida slowly appeared in front of them. She sparkled, smiled and reached out her watery hands. Her hands gently covered their hands. She held them silently for a moment, then slowly guided them up.

They shot out of the river with such force! The couple held onto each other's hands tightly as water rushed about them. They felt ground beneath their feet and stood; they were still encompassed with water but Aida -and Marcouera's presence- was gone.

Face to face, they stood, looking intently at one another. Water continued to surround them. Suddenly their hands sparked with a flash of light, and they let go. The magic was gone. They stood empty handed and out of breath, looking around for what they had just seen.

With a jolt, Mara saw they were back on top of the Great Falls. As a marhilia, she would not have questioned the ability to go up or down with water, but as a human, it felt very unnatural.

Cyrus steadied himself as he, too, realized where they were.

They both searched their hands for traces of the river's sand, shimmer, and crystals. They looked for Marcouera but she was gone and they knew it.

The final surge of ancient power had been used.

40 Forged

The columns had been delivered into the stands. In that same moment when Mara and Cyrus were elevated back to the top of the rocks at the falls, the ancient magic of Maracoeura flashed throughout the land. The entire new irrigation system glowed! Column ends magically adhered to one another and the stands were forged tight to them, making the new structure one solid piece.

Gone were the sticks and branches and in their places were solid marble with streaks of white, blue and silver. The white columns were one long, stable trough.

The blue glow reached all the corners of the land. Enchantment filled the air.

The river's origin was now from the mountains of Mardivina and from this day forth it would only flow in one direction. The change had begun when Mara's transformation started, but now it was final. No traces of the Slow Current remained; the river was left with one current only.

The blue crystal ribbons flashed, whipped and shot to the bottom of the river, burying themselves in the river rock. Marhilias fell into the river and faded into water. The sprites were gone now, only water remained.

Except for one.

Aida, who had experienced a transformation of her own, in a way. She had felt a touch of strength, a bit of power, and some small magic in her remained. She had felt all the world around her die. She knew the magic of the water kingdom was gone and she felt heavy with the weight of this knowledge. The crystals were no more, their ancient magic had been used. Marcouera no longer called her, the river was silent and she was alone.

The last marhilia.

41 Watering Changes

Over the weeks and months that followed, watering tasks were divided among the citizens of Terramara. The map that Mara and Cyrus had created was kept in the palace library. Their irrigation system was checked daily and people hauled water from the great trough to the corners of the desert and plains.

Plans were made to make smaller systems, to draw water to more corners where it was needed. This time, they would use wood. The massive main structure was formidable and covered all of Terramara. Still, there was work to be done in getting water to all living things.

The people of Terramara thrived in their new roles, learning about the flow of water, and caring for the farms and fruit trees on their own. They seemed to have a natural affinity for it. They found immense joy in growing and producing their own food and keeping their land green.

Time went on and the lands, fields and plants thrived. Aida watched from her watery perch. Mixed feelings filled her as she watched the humans water. She envied their excitement- they were thrilled watching things grow- a joy that used to be singularly marhilias'.

She floated alone to Cazmel. The river that ran through the forest used to bring her so much joy. She crawled up her favorite tree. Large and comforting, she sat brooding on its branches, her orange ripple glowing. Aida wondered what it was like to be human. She had seen Mara many times, but now with her human eyes, Aida's tiny form was often missed.

She wondered when she would disappear like the

rest of the marhilias had. She put that thought out of her head and decided to visit her oldest friend instead. Neither of them knew how much time she had left in Terramara, so why waste a moment? She floated on toward the white castle.

42 Watering

Relief and joy washed over Mara each night as she marveled at Terramara's transformation. Their task was being accomplished. The world was surviving beautifully.

One evening, before the sun went down, they joined some friends at the waterfalls for a refreshing dip. As Johatt, Lila and others took swan dives off the ledge, Mara held Cyrus back.

He smiled and regarded his partner with love. "What is it?" he asked.

"Just look at this land," Mara began with pride. "Look at the columns. Water is everywhere."

Ivory troughs stood shining and tall, stretching as far as they could see in any one direction.

Cyrus joined her with a huge grin. "Yes, it's wonderful. We did it. It's all working out amazingly well. We could not hope for more!"

"Well, maybe," Mara hinted mysteriously.

Cyrus gave her a quizzical look. She laughed and hit him playfully on the shoulder.

"Let's dive in!"

She held back for a moment and watched his strong legs stride off the rocks, smiling as her hands went instinctively to her belly.   Mara would tell him soon that a baby was on the way.

But tonight, she would swim with her new friends, in her new world, thankful for the love she had found and for Terramara thriving under her care.

Author Bio

Kris Fuller is an author, artist and inspirational speaker. She loves writing and poetry is one of her favourite things. She is the CEO of Your Life Sparkles and Co-Creative Chair of the Best Ever You Network and she believes everyone should follow their dreams, love themselves more and be kind to others.

Kris has taught and consulted in public education in England, Ontario, Alberta and British Columbia. Kris is a graduate of the University of Alberta (Bachelor of Education) and University of Sedona (Bachelor of Metaphysics).

Kris lives in Enderby, BC with her cat, Mia. They love sunsets, fires and a curling up with a good book.

Learn more about Kris Fuller:

krisfullerauthor.com
@krisfullerauthor on Facebook

krisfullerart.com
@krisfullerfine on Facebook

yourlifesparkles.com
@yourlifesparkles.com on Facebook and Instagram

CPSIA information can be obtained
at www.ICGtesting.com
Printed in the USA
BVHW080055231020
591567BV00001B/22

9 781649 214638